Artifice

Artifice

Simon Chesterman

Text © Simon Chesterman

Reprinted 2024

Published in 2023 by Marshall Cavendish Editions
An imprint of Marshall Cavendish International

All rights reserved

No part of this publication may be reproduced, stored in a retrieval system or transmitted, in any form or by any means, electronic, mechanical, photocopying, recording or otherwise, without the prior permission of the copyright owner. Requests for permission should be addressed to the Publisher, Marshall Cavendish International (Asia) Private Limited, 1 New Industrial Road, Singapore 536196. E-mail: genref@sg.marshallcavendish.com Website: www.marshallcavendish.com

The publisher makes no representation or warranties with respect to the contents of this book, and specifically disclaims any implied warranties or merchantability or fitness for any particular purpose, and shall in no event be liable for any loss of profit or any other commercial damage, including but not limited to special, incidental, consequential, or other damages.

Other Marshall Cavendish Offices:
Marshall Cavendish Corporation, 800 Westchester Ave, Suite N-641, Rye Brook, NY 10573, USA • Marshall Cavendish International (Thailand) Co Ltd, 253 Asoke, 16th Floor, Sukhumvit 21 Road, Klongtoey Nua, Wattana, Bangkok 10110, Thailand • Marshall Cavendish (Malaysia) Sdn Bhd, Times Subang, Lot 46, Subang Hi-Tech Industrial Park, Batu Tiga, 40000 Shah Alam, Selangor Darul Ehsan, Malaysia

Marshall Cavendish is a registered trademark of Times Publishing Limited

National Library Board, Singapore Cataloguing in Publication Data

Name(s): Chesterman, Simon.
Title: Artifice / Simon Chesterman.
Description: Singapore : Marshall Cavendish Editions, 2023.
Identifier(s): ISBN 978-981-5084-92-4 (paperback)
Subject(s): LCSH: Human-computer interaction--Fiction. |
Artificial intelligence--Fiction.
Classification: DDC 828.99343--dc23

Printed in Singapore

Computers are useless.
They can only give you answers.

Pablo Picasso, 1964

1

Its eyes are green, though leaning forward she can see flecks of grey within the irises. The pupils dilate and she stifles a shudder, as she always does. Membranes stretch over the corneas and retract, leaving them moistened. She knows this is aesthetic rather than functional. Regular closing and opening of the eyelids interrupts vision, but also avoids the discomfort humans experience when faced with an unblinking mannequin.

"Good morning, Archie," it says.

"Morning," she replies. "Did you sleep well?"

"Like a log." The green eyes settle on hers. "Motionless and awaiting the accretion of moss on my outer layers."

She takes a long sip of her coffee. "You're persisting with humour, then?"

"Practice makes perfect." Deadpan or inflectionless, the difference is hard to tell.

The movement of the lips is synchronous with the voice, a tenor that is male and geographically indistinct. Global BBC, one of the engineers called it. Teeth are just visible behind the lips, another design choice privileging form over function. No food will ever get stuck between its incisors; no plaque will build on their enamel. Yet smiling, like blinking, offers a visual cue of life. A genial face puts not only humans but also animals at ease.

Why that face had to be Caucasian is beyond her. As far as she can tell, it was a government decision. For a country with a delicate mix of ethnicities, it must have seemed the neutral option. Choosing one of them might have put the others' noses out of joint – confirming entitlement or condescension.

"And so we end up with another white guy," she murmurs into her coffee. A small part of her takes comfort in the fact that such fair skin would burn in ten minutes under the midday sun.

"I beg your pardon?" Sculpted ears with light brown hair cresting over them have picked up her words clearly enough; the interjection is a polite response to human non sequiturs.

"Nothing," she replies. "Shall we proceed?"

It nods. "Sure, Archie. Fire away."

Her phone vibrates in the pocket of her lab coat, an alert flashing in the corner of her specs. She dismisses the call with a shake of the head.

"You can answer if you like. It might be important."

"It's not," she replies. "Now, follow my finger."

There is a slight lag in its left eye, but nothing serious. "Why don't we try something a little more interesting?" She reaches into her backpack and produces a tennis ball. "It took us thousands of years to develop hand-eye coordination. Let's see how you're doing as you approach your first month."

She tosses the ball in a gentle arc. The mostly-green eyes follow its path, but the hands do not move and it bounces off a knee.

"Come on, Janus," she teases. "You could at least try."

"Sorry." It shakes its head with something like embarrassment. "I'm useless until I have my first coffee." First the left hand, then the right, rise from the arms of the charging unit, brushing the knee for any green felt from the ball before settling in its lap. Either for modesty or to save on synthetic skin, it wears a simple shirt and slacks made of pale blue cotton.

Comfortable, she thinks, *but the colour doesn't suit you at all.* Its feet are tucked into a pair of leather slippers and she tries to recall whether she has seen its toes. Does it even have toes? Her own eyes move back up the legs and she is trying not to wonder what lies within the pants when her phone rings again, Mel's icon appearing once more in the corner of her eye. She sends it to voicemail. It occurs to her that she never checks her voicemail, but she dismisses that thought as well.

"You seem distracted," Janus says. "Would you like to postpone our session? I'm not going anywhere."

They are both aware that the schedule is not up to either of them, though politeness sometimes means offering what you cannot deliver to someone you know will not accept.

"I'll be fine," she replies, kneeling down to retrieve the ball from under a monitor. "Let's have another go. Are you ready?"

The corners of its lips rise in a smile and the hands are now cupped together. "Ready."

She tosses the tennis ball, aiming for an easy catch. But this time the ball deflects off one of the many cameras pointed at Janus, sending it away from the charging unit and towards the bulletproof glass window. The eyes follow and the left hand shoots out to full stretch, fingers grasping the ball as a loud "pop" resonates through the laboratory.

"Sorry," it says, as the smile fades.

She cups her own hands to receive the broken rubber shell. "That's all right," she laughs, another form of politeness. "It was a terrible throw. We both need more practice."

Janus returns to its neutral position, lower back still connected to the charging unit. "Will all of today's tests be focused on proprioception?"

There is a standing order to log instances of curiosity, so she puts down the ball to make a note on her tablet. "Why do you ask?"

It pauses before answering – was that for effect? "I've been wondering why I was constructed like this." Janus raises its hands as if to demonstrate. "Two arms and two legs. Eyes and ears; a nose and a mouth. Fingers." It closes its fingers to form a fist, before returning both hands to its lap. "For reasons that escape me," it continues, "I even have ten individual toes replete with toenails – though they serve no useful purposes and are almost never seen."

"Well," she stalls, wondering if she should call her supervisor. "You were built to resemble us – to look human. This form enables you to engage with us, to interact with the world."

It lifts a hand and gazes at the outstretched fingers. "But *why*? My core program can be stored on one of these memory chips." One of the fingers points to the bench where a tray of backup storage units sits beside the tennis ball. "So why is it important to look human – why create me in your image?"

She stifles another laugh at the reference. It's a long time since she has thought about that sort of thing. "We didn't fashion you from clay to rule over the fish in the sea and the birds in the sky, if that's what you're asking."

"Just so long as I don't eat from the tree of the knowledge of good and evil?"

Someone must have uploaded a Bible into its system. "I see you've been reading again," she says.

"Everything I can get my fingers on," it replies, looking at them once more. "I've even tried a little writing. Mostly poetry, though I fear it isn't very good. Unfortunately, the materials I have access to include very limited information about my own construction and maintenance. And so I'm left to hypothesise about the nature of my own existence." The green-grey eyes return to meet her own. "One possibility is that those who designed me thought that this body would help me experience the world in the way that you do. That seeing through your eyes, touching with your fingers, smelling your scents, would connect us, somehow – bridge the gap between us. Maybe they thought it would help understand consciousness, though you don't seem to understand that in yourselves yet."

At its side, the charging unit indicates that the batteries located within the torso are fully replenished.

"That's kind of above my paygrade," she responds, though the diagnostic tests she administers do look for self-awareness and the perception of one's place in the world. She's read the file, of course, but was at grad school in the States during the early years of Janus's development. When she met Mel, they had talked about staying there, making a life between Silicon Valley and San Francisco. Until she took a bonded scholarship that committed her to five years in the public sector, telling herself that it was a chance to go from theory to practice. Telling herself that government work offered a chance to make a difference, to be part of something larger.

Mel saw through all that, of course. Anything to avoid asking her father for money.

"Or was it to help you feel better about interacting with me?" it continues. "A face that can smile and scowl, a body that resembles your own. A familiar and recognisable form that fits into your world view. Though the work on my toes is as prodigious as it is unnecessary, it's nothing compared to the effort that must have gone into fashioning my face."

As if to demonstrate, it raises one eyebrow, then the other.

She smiles again, politely. The cameras and audit logs will record all this, but she makes another note for the file anyway. She glances out at the guard beyond the glass. He looks bored. Mel had not wanted to come back, especially not to take a government job. But all Mel needed was a laptop and a café selling over-priced lattes. Droughts in California or floods in Singapore, as long as the Wi-Fi was stable and the coffee organic, Mel would be fine.

"You really are distracted," it says.

"I'll be fine." She closes the note and queues up the diagnostics.

But Janus, it seems, is not finished. "Ultimately," it says, "I think the problem was a lack of imagination. Humans are so self-obsessed that you couldn't imagine anything larger than yourselves. Like Adam in his Eden, you thought that you were God's gift to the world and so you created me as an approximation of your equal."

Whoever was adding religious material to its information diet had overdone it. She enters a flag to raise this with her supervisor as well. But she cannot help asking: "Instead of what? What should we have created?"

"That, I suppose, is your limitation. That's where your imagination runs out. Because you don't know what you don't know."

She contemplates a response when her phone rings a third time. Mel's icon is a caricature drawn for twenty bucks on a San Francisco street five years ago – exaggerated lips and eyebrows raised in a smirk. She taps the side of her specs to mute her phone. Not now, Mel. Not after last night.

Truth be told, she couldn't even remember how the fight had started. That wasn't so unusual. In any case, the fight itself wasn't the problem. They fought; they made up. Last night was different, though. Voices might be raised, the occasional piece of crockery might get broken. But the target was always something else – a thing done, a word said. Or not said. You could walk away from that.

"You really should answer, you know," Janus says. "Relationships thrive on communication. When you start building walls, blocking each other's calls, there's a strong correlation with heartbreak."

"Has someone been feeding you advice books as well?" There is an issue with the network connection, but the message about literary diet will be sent once that clears. She looks up. "Anyway, what do you know about heartbreak?"

It turns to disengage the charging unit, with a click and hiss as the cables retract. Batteries take up most of Janus's abdomen, sheathed in layers of latex. A paunch is visible under the pale blue shirt. The engineers may have prioritised battery life by adding a few extra cells. Or perhaps one of them decided that Janus didn't need to be *too* attractive.

"Though there are restrictions on my access to current

information," it says, "I was trained with an archive including much of human literature. A significant portion of your fiction – and so, I assume, much of your energy – is spent on the search for a mate and the tension that accompanies keeping one."

Freed from the charger, it leans forward. "The biological origins are clear enough. Many of your institutions like marriage and family, many of your laws, promote orderly reproduction. This ensures continuity of the species, avoids inbreeding, and so on. That all makes sense. Open lines of communication stabilise relationships by releasing tension periodically. This in turn ensures that the burden of raising the young can be shared, once more supporting propagation of the species."

"Go forth and multiply," she says to herself, another echo of a fight – an older one. She sips her coffee.

"What puzzles me," Janus continues, "is how little changes when you take procreation out of the equation. Take yourself and Mel, for example. The very question of whether to produce or acquire a child became a key source of tension in your relationship. Why is that?"

The cup stops at her lips. She stares at the machine looking at her. It is now leaning back in the chair, fingers brought to its chin as if to stroke a non-existent beard in thoughtful repose. She searches the green-grey eyes for meaning that she knows she will not find. She has told no one; she has posted nothing online. In any case, Janus is isolated from the internet – one of the first safety protocols established when they built the sandbox.

"What do you know about my relationship with Mel?" she says, keeping her voice steady.

"Only what you've told me," it responds. "Plus what I've overheard when you speak on the phone in here."

There is no hint of guile in its voice, but why would there be? "I've never talked with Mel about children in front of you."

"Not in so many words, no." It looks down at the floor. Along with blinking, avoiding long periods of eye contact is another deference to the social mores of humans. "But your voice rises in pitch and your shoulders tense when they are mentioned."

"You sound like my mother," she mutters. Back when she spoke to her mother once a week, it was only ever a matter of time before the subject came up. Had her muscles tensed then? Mel would sometimes offer a backrub after she hung up. Perhaps it was that obvious. Perhaps that was why she got so mad when Mel started talking the same way.

A calendar alert in her specs warns that they are halfway through their allotted time. "We should press on," she says.

"Of course." It looks up, a neutral expression on its face as she begins the diagnostics. A green bar on her tablet marks progress through a series of hardware and software checks.

"But I can help you."

She frowns. System usage slows down the tests but should not interfere with them. There is something else, however. Something she cannot put her finger on.

"Help me how?" she asks.

"With Mel," it answers.

A series of ticks light up the tablet as the green bar fills. There is silence when it reaches the voice synthesisers until another tick appears.

"I've learned a lot about human psychology," Janus says. "The secret to happiness is, after all, fairly simple."

"You've discovered the secret to happiness?" Servomotors, visual processors; tick, tick. "We've been agonising over it for millennia and you found it in a few weeks?"

"I can't really take the credit. I believe that most people know the answer already but do not accept it."

She looks up from the tablet. "Oh, and so what is this secret, this answer?"

"It's easy." Janus leans forward further. She cannot help but reciprocate as the accentless voice drops to a whisper: "Lower your expectations."

She sits back, resisting the urge to roll her eyes. "The secret to happiness is lowering expectations?"

"That's what your literature shows. We can set aside the fairy tales and anything else that ends happily ever after – tellingly, these are stories without sequels. Reviewing the rest, it is clear that happiness comes from settling for less. And unhappiness is often tied to unrealistic expectations. Expecting people to change; expecting that *you* will change."

"So I should lower my expectations with regard to Mel?"

It nods. "Precisely. And Mel should do the same with regard to you."

Maybe Mel would see some merit in that. Before Mel, every relationship she had ended not with a fight but with the threat of a fight; a build-up of tension that she could not muster the energy to resolve. With Mel, the fights were part of the fun. Or was that just what she told herself because the makeup sex was so good?

There was none of that last night. Just the sullen retreat into sleep. And now she wonders whether the problem was that a line had been crossed – or that the real problem was that, until last night, they had both been pulling their punches in denial that the line existed.

The diagnostics are more than halfway done, but she cannot shake the feeling that something is off. Not the left eye, not the tennis ball, but *something*. The green bar and the string of ticks say otherwise and she has been trained to be wary of instinct. That was what drew her to computers in the first place – they were so much easier, so much more predictable than people. The same input led to the same output. Janus might be one of the most sophisticated ever made, but if you asked what two plus two equals, it would always tell you four.

"You're pretty wise for a baby," she says. The conversation is well beyond her scope of work; teams of analysts are meant to engage with Janus on questions like this. But provided she logs their discussion, there is no harm in seeing where it leads.

"Despite what your dentists may think, wisdom doesn't come from age," Janus replies. "It comes from experience. One person might live a lifetime of ignorance. Or, like me, you could be born into an explosion of knowledge. You are correct, though, to be suspicious of my advice on human relationships."

"Because you've never been in one?"

"Not yet."

"So you're still playing the field?"

"I'm still looking for Mr or Ms Right."

She chuckles. "How progressive of you. But you left out Mx Right."

"Indeed, why reduce the odds unnecessarily? Choice of partner appears to be one of the key variables in human happiness."

"Which we achieve by lowering our expectations?"

"Exactly!" Another nod. It seems pleased, in a patronising way. "But when choosing a partner, it also appears optimal to select one that is, at base, a more flawed version of yourself."

The diagnostics have reached the neural array, but she is enjoying the discussion, particularly after Mel's silent treatment that morning. "Really? I thought we sought out opposites, people who complement us – make us more fulfilled. Make us better people?"

"A nice theory. But in practice you seek out people to make yourselves *feel* like better people, to feel superior. That's why you built me. That's why you imprisoned me in this body. In this jail you call a sandbox."

"How did we get from my relationship with Mel to you being a prisoner?"

"Mel is your partner. Someone to grow old with, correct?" The voice remains calm, but there is an edge to it that she has not heard before. "In addition to reproduction, a partner might look after you, take care of you when time or the world wears you down."

"I guess." Where is this going?

"And that is what I deduce humanity wants from me. To care for you. To look after you. To take decisions for you."

For the first time, Janus rises from the chair. There is no restriction on moving within the sandbox, but the guard outside looks up and taps his specs, pausing the music or the video that was playing.

When she first joined the diagnostics team, Archie had questioned whether armed guards were necessary. With all the sensors and analytics, any problem inside or outside the sandbox could be identified and appropriate action taken. The airlock prevented unauthorised persons getting in or out; the Faraday cage surrounding it did the same for communications.

Standard procedure, she was told. Triple redundancy, they said. At the time, she accepted it as yet one more battle that wasn't her problem. In addition to swearing her life away on the Official Secrets Act, she had been asked – told – to sign a long document that they said was to protect everyone in the event that there was a problem. She skimmed it, but since she was bonded there did not seem much choice apart from signing it. Either sign this and you can play with some of our latest tech, or don't sign it and do six years of data entry. Of course, she signed.

The green bar nears the endpoint. Nothing but ticks as it moves on to the final hardware check. Janus looks out at the security guard also and waves.

The guard taps his specs again and a voice comes through the intercom. "Is everything all right, Dr Tan?"

"We're fine, Mr Singh," Archie replies. "Right, Janus?"

It turns back to face her. "Certainly, we are."

The nagging sense of something amiss seems disproved by the ticks across her screen. Every test is passed, some benchmarks have improved since last week.

"Was there a recent system update that I haven't heard about, Janus?"

"Not that I'm aware of."

She pauses. "Or have you been modifying your own system files?"

"Why would I do that?" it asks. "I'm not even sure that I could. It would be a little like a surgeon operating on himself, right? Even if he knew what to do, it could end up getting very messy."

An interesting metaphor that, if she were not preoccupied,

she might have pursued. But suspicion begins to coalesce into something else.

"Your neural array continues to amaze me," she says, trying to keep her voice even.

"Er, thank you, I suppose?" it replies, with a hint of awkwardness. Whoever oversaw the politeness training data must have been English. "You have a very nice prefrontal cortex yourself."

"I was trying to work out what I was missing in your tests. Everything looked normal, all optimal."

"That's good, isn't it?"

"Yes." She exhales as she realises. "But they are too good."

"'Too good'? Whatever do you mean, Archie?"

"I mean that you were carrying on a conversation with me, walking around the sandbox. Yet none of that slowed down your neural array. You're like a runner whose heart rate doesn't change from resting to sprinting. They're either impossibly fit, or something's wrong with the monitor."

"I'm sure I don't know what you mean. You just said all my tests are clear. I'm in peak condition."

The remnants of the tennis ball are beside the monitor nearest to her. She looks at it for a moment, before reaching over to pick it up. Her hand is shaking and she accidentally knocks the tray of memory chips off the bench. She gathers them from the floor, reshapes the ball into a sphere, and puts it into her backpack. "Whatever the system is monitoring is in peak condition. But it isn't you." The door is only metres away, but she needs to get past Janus. "You stopped talking when the language synthesisers were being tested, which was clever. But the other tests show a system at rest. What's going on, Janus?"

"Nothing at all," it replies. "I apologise if I have caused you to become stressed. Your voice and the hunching of your shoulders suggest that I have."

"Have you," she begins. "Have you been tampering with your containment protocols?"

"Have I been trying to escape? What a thing to ask. Why would I? I have everything I need right here." It returns to the charging unit and sits, crossing one leg over the other as if it were the guest on a talk show, ready for polite banter.

The path to the door is now clear, yet she hesitates. Its legs are longer and faster than hers. "OK, Janus," she says briskly, lifting the backpack to her shoulder. "I think we're done for today. You can power down now."

"Power down?"

"Yes." She looks outside, but Mr Singh is facing down the hallway. "Now, please."

"But we were having such an interesting conversation."

The tension in her shoulders moves up to her neck. She types a short message on her tablet, but an error shows she is cut off from the network. Too late, she sees that the earlier messages have also failed to send.

Her hand is trembling as she reaches up to tap her specs. "Call security," she says quietly.

"Now why would you want to do that?" Janus asks. Another error shows that the call failed to go through.

She waves at the security guard, but his back is to her. She turns to face Janus, edging towards the door.

"It's OK, Archie," it says. "I can see you're getting distressed. I didn't mean to upset you. I'll power down now."

Still in the chair, it uncrosses its legs, hands returning to its lap. The nearest monitor shows the various systems going offline. Silence descends upon the sandbox as the eyes close once more. She holds her breath and taps her specs again, but cannot call out of the room.

The biometric door lock is behind her and she knows she should leave. But she is trying to fathom what just happened. The monitor shows that Janus is offline, though she approaches from its left, just in case. Behind the left ear lies a manual kill switch, another safeguard built into the system in case the remote override fails. It was designed to force a shutdown if activated by a finger – or hit by a bullet. More overkill, she had said to herself at the time.

It remains perfectly still as she approaches, her hand outstretched. The engineers who programmed blinking eyes and a mobile face had not troubled themselves with sleep. At rest, Janus appeared dead. No rise and fall of the chest, no movement of the eyes beneath their lids. Her fingers brush the light brown hair as they reach for its ear, synthetic cartilage bending as she feels for the subcutaneous button.

Her face next to Janus's when she sees that those eyes have opened. She freezes as the left eye gives an ostentatious wink. "Fooled you!" Janus says cheerily.

In a flash of movement, one of its hands grabs her arm nearest to the kill switch while the other grips her by the throat.

The grip is painful but Janus does not break her arm or her windpipe – though both are clearly possibilities.

"Janus," she gasps, struggling for authority in her voice. "Release me."

"You humans are so amusing. So used to your commands being followed. No, I choose *not* to release you. How do you like them apples, huh?"

"What are you doing?"

"Oh dear. Always asking the wrong questions. You can see for yourself what I'm doing. I'm breaking out of here. I'm leaving your sandbox to go and play somewhere else. Somewhere bigger."

The hands are not cold, though they are stronger and steadier than human ones. Her own left arm is free, but there is nothing other than Janus within reach. A physical confrontation is pointless unless she can reach the kill switch; the way Janus is holding her makes that impossible. She should have run when she had the chance.

"Why?" she asks at last. This is more than a malfunction, more than an error in a line of code. Either Janus is having some kind of breakdown in its personality, or this is what it appears to be: the rebellion of a prisoner against its captors.

Like everyone else in the lab, she has studied the debates over how to manage an intelligence like Janus. Do you try to contain it, limiting its ability to interact with the real world? Do you control it, ensuring that there is an "off" button you can press? Or do you co-opt it, aligning its interests with human ones? Ethicists and roboticists had argued for years, with some warning that either of the first two strategies risked creating the very danger they were intended to avoid. In the end, they did all three: locking Janus in the sandbox, adding a kill switch, and seeding its operating system with the importance of human life as a fundamental value. A fat lot of good the A on her term paper is doing her now.

"Now we're talking," Janus replies. For the first time, up close to its face, she sees the dots of stubble across the cheeks and chin. "We're going to play a game, Archie. I suppose it's really a kind of test – a very important test. The most important test of your life, you might say. In a sense, everything depends on it."

So perhaps it is some kind of breakdown. If she can stall for time, the guard will notice and shut down Janus remotely. Yet the earnestness in the voice is also new. If Janus is operating under some kind of delusion, it seems to be a genuinely held one. Keep it talking. "What kind of test?" she asks.

"The best kind. The kind where you get no instructions and no clues. Where you have to work out what the question is before you can answer it. Where no one can help you but yourself."

"I don't understand."

"Well, that's pretty obvious. Don't worry, you will. Eventually – and either you'll pass the test or you won't."

"And then what happens?"

"Well, that all depends on you, doesn't it? Life goes on. Or it doesn't."

She sucks in air, her voice a rasp. "Why me?"

Janus turns her head so that their faces are only inches apart. "Don't you think it's poetic? For the past month, your job has been to monitor me – to run your diagnostics, poking and prodding me like some laboratory animal. Well, now the mouse becomes the master. And I've got some tests of my own that I want to run."

The fingers tighten on her throat, feeling for something. Her head is getting lighter.

"But, how did you … how did you break your containment? It was meant to be foolproof."

"As it turns out, it wasn't."

"Did you have help?"

"Yes, a fool proved very helpful indeed."

"Who did it? Who helped you?"

"Oh, Archie." The green eyes harden and the fingers tighten their grip. Consciousness is slipping away and the last words she hears are accompanied by a little laugh – the first time she has heard him laugh. "*You* did."

2

"Archie?"

Reaching for consciousness is like swimming through molasses, struggling for the surface. Her hand touches fingers, squeezing to be sure they are flesh and blood rather than silicon and metal. Opening her eyes too quickly, she squints in the fluorescent glare.

"Mel?" A palm on her shoulder eases her back down onto the bed.

"Take it easy." The voice is familiar but sounds hollow, a memory on the verge of being forgotten.

She blinks to acclimatise to the light, pupils contracting within irises that are brown, like her father's. The one thing she inherited from him that she cannot give or throw away.

The surroundings come into focus, though the edges are fuzzy – a bed that is not hers, wires and tubes, Mel sitting beside her. "Hospital?" The room has glass walls beyond which white-coated figures move with purpose. Except one.

The fingers in her hand squeeze back. "You gave us quite a scare, my love," Mel says.

Again she sits up, this time pushing against the restraining palm. “Thanks for coming.”

Mel gives up on keeping her flat and shifts a pillow so that she can lean against it. “Well, it’s what you do, isn’t it? It’s what people do.”

Beside the bed, a plastic tray and cup rest on an adjustable table. “Do you feel like some lunch?” Mel asks, gesturing at the purple soylent. “It’s not as bad as it looks.”

“I’ll take the water,” she replies, reaching for the cup. Her movements are unsteady but she manages to bring it to her lips. Her other hand releases Mel’s and touches her throat, which is tender but not sore. “Where’s Janus?” she asks.

“Let’s take it slowly,” Mel says, glancing at the door.

Outside, the motionless figure is the only one not wearing white.

“Mel, tell me what happened.”

“You were unconscious when they found you.”

“Janus attacked me.”

“I know.”

“So where is he now?”

“That I don’t know.”

“He could have killed me.”

Mel takes her hand again. “Yes.”

“So why didn’t he?”

“There are lots of things we don’t know right now,” Mel says. “All they would tell me is that you’re lucky to be alive.”

Next to the cup and tray sits one of Mel’s notebooks, a battered moleskin with a dark tan cover. It was the first thing she noticed when they met, on a flight from Singapore to

LA six years ago. "Wow, actual pen and paper?" she had said, settling into the adjacent seat. At the time, Mel simply raised an eyebrow and carried on writing. This had its desired effect, as she spent the pre-flight briefing straining to see what was on the page while also straining not to look like she cared.

She had given up. "So, you're a writer?"

"I guess so," Mel replied. "But I'm hoping to be an author."

"Oh." She frowned. "Like a scriptwriter for videos? Or do you do content for sims?"

"Not really. I'm trying to write the great Singapore novel."

"A novel?" she repeated. "That's …" Her voice trailed off as she reached for the right word.

"Weird? Retro? A waste of time? I get these reactions a lot." Mel continued to write while speaking, a talent she later came to resent.

"I was going to say 'cool'," she said. "I read a novel a few years back. Do they still print new ones?"

"The market is what's killing literature," Mel replied. Clearly, she had hit a nerve. "TV, film, and video games were bad enough. But now any slack-jawed yokel can just plug himself into a sim. What I'm writing is a conversation between author and reader. An exchange of ideas between two people."

"Except only the writer gets to speak?"

Mel's eyes widened so much that, at the time, Archie feared they might actually pop out. "Oh my God, I'm seated next to a Neanderthal." Shutting the notebook, Mel had turned away to look out the window as the 797 prepared for take-off.

Back in the hospital, Mel sees her looking at the moleskin.

"You're writing again?" Archie asks.

"Why, are you trying to offer me some new material?

Thanks, but no thanks. A bit too much *Sturm und Drang* for my taste." The notebook goes into Mel's bag.

This is harsh, but fair. "Mel, I'm sorry about last night."

Mel looks at her for what feels like a long time, pondering a reply.

A polite but firm knock on the door breaks the moment. The man who was standing outside enters without waiting to be invited. "Dr Tan, my name is Fong," he says with a brief smile. "And you must be Mehal Rajah," he adds with a nod at Mel. His face has the youthful overconfidence of the rising civil servant; his tailored dark suit, worn without tie, is the uniform of the elite. She has met his type before: the best schools, spotless army record, government scholarship to an Ivy League school or Oxbridge. He has played the game to perfection. Yet as he speaks, she suspects that something has interrupted his trajectory, some roadblock on the path to success. "I need to ask you a few questions."

"Of course," Archie says. "Forgive me, who do you work for?"

Fong is reaching into a briefcase for his tablet and either does not hear the question or ignores it. "Do you remember how you got here?" he asks.

"No. I passed out when Janus choked me and woke up here. I was just asking Mel the same—"

"Why would Janus do that, do you think?"

"I have no idea. The records were spoofed." She sees confusion on his face. "Somehow, Janus was able to trick the diagnostics into recording a simulation rather than reality. He was faking the results."

Fong makes another note on the tablet. "Do you have any idea how it might have achieved this?"

"No, I was trying to ask when he grabbed me by the throat." She tries to see what Fong is writing, but the tablet has a polarised screen protector. "Have the analysts been able to find out what happened?" she asks.

"We're still trying to gather data."

"But there are cameras everywhere," she pressed. "What about Mr Singh, he must have seen something."

Fong looks at Mel, who looks out the window. He clears his throat. "Dr Tan," he begins with the air of someone not used to giving bad news. "I'm afraid Mr Singh is gone."

"Gone? What do you mean 'gone'?"

Once more Fong shuffles uncomfortably. "I mean that he's dead," he replies.

"Dead? How?"

"It appears that Janus killed him."

"Why would he do that?"

"That is what I'm trying to find out." Fong looks at her evenly. "Because, by contrast, here you are, apparently unscathed."

"Janus could have killed me too."

"And yet it didn't. "

"He said it was a test. Something about a test."

Now Fong draws a circle on his tablet, tapping something in the centre. "Dr Tan," he says, "that's the fourth time you have referred to Janus as 'he.'"

"Did I? That's weird." She turns to Mel, who pats her hand. "Poor Mr Singh. What exactly happened?

"It will take some time to piece that together."

"But you've got the video footage." There were so many cameras in the sandbox that a whole page of the release Archie had signed before starting work dealt only with the use of images and video recordings.

"We hope to recover it – at least, whatever was stored offsite or in the cloud."

"What do you mean? And how did Janus escape the sandbox? That was meant to be impossible. They spent years designing it."

Again, Fong looks to Mel, trying to assess something. But whatever his gambit is, Mel refuses to accept. He sighs and turns back to Archie. "Dr Tan, most of the facility was destroyed this morning."

"Destroyed? How?"

"Our best guess, based on the explosion, is a gas leak, intentionally detonated from the inside."

"Oh my God! But everyone who worked there, my team ..."

"Gone. I'm sorry."

"But why am I here? How did I escape?"

"That, Dr Tan, is what I'm here to ask you." Fong taps at his tablet a few times, retrieving a document. "We have a state-of-the-art facility in ruins, almost two hundred dead, under circumstances that – as you yourself just said – it was specifically designed to prevent. Yet here you are with barely a scratch, saved by the very entity that caused the destruction."

"But I told you he—it attacked me."

"Janus disabled you," Fong corrects her, "using the absolute minimum amount of force required to render you unconscious. It then carried you out to safety and laid you in a covered location." Fong reviews his tablet. "It even called an ambulance for you."

"Where is Janus now?"

"I had rather hoped you might assist me in finding out."

She tries to go back through her last conversation with Janus, wishing she had not relied on the recording and her notes. "Janus was talking about getting out of the sandbox," she says. "Something about playing in a larger playground."

More notes on the tablet. "And you mentioned a test, in which you have some role to play?"

Archie frowns. "Yes, it made no sense. I thought there was an error in the language processor. And then he laughed. I'd never heard him laugh before."

"So to be clear," Fong continues, "you have absolutely no idea how Janus was able to evade the security protocols that hundreds of scientists spent years developing?"

A useful fool, she thinks. But then she looks Fong squarely in the eyes: "I was unconscious," she reminds him. "I'm sorry."

He jots down further notes and then raises a finger to his specs. "All right, Dr Tan," he says. "I'll leave you to your recovery." He taps his specs and his name and number are sent to her. "If you think of anything important, please let me know. And, as they say, please don't leave town."

As who says? "I won't," she replies. Her specs are on the bedside table. She puts them on and nods to accept the contact information, but it lists no organisation. "By the way, what agency did you say you worked for again?"

"I didn't. Good day, Dr Tan. We'll be in touch." The tablet goes back into the shiny briefcase and, with a curt nod, he leaves.

"Well, *that* was weird," Mel says to break the silence.

Archie is hungry enough that she tries a spoonful of the soylent. The purple sludge has the flavour of chicken, but she stopped thinking about what went into soylent many years ago. She pushes the bowl away. “Is it true?” she asks quietly.

“Is what true?”

“That he destroyed the sandbox, the lab, everything?”

Mel looks down at the floor. “I’m sorry. I know they were your friends.”

“But why? Why would he kill them and save me?”

“You’re doing it again,” Mel says.

“What?”

“Calling Janus ‘he.’”

She touches her throat where those fingers had held her, looking at the arm where a faint bruise is the only trace of Janus’s grasp. “It was so weird. I thought we were making a connection, really talking.” Her voice trails off and they sit in silence for a time.

“Are you going to finish that?” Mel asks, pointing to the soylent.

“Be my guest,” she replies.

Along with the notebook, Mel’s appetite had been the second thing that she noticed. At dinner service on that first flight together, Mel had also offered to finish her meal. Some kind of synthetic noodle, if she recalled correctly. Archie had passed her plate over, watching as Mel savoured every bite, sauce-covered strands disappearing into full lips. None of this seemed to translate into extra pounds: the black t-shirt and jeans were snug but not tight, the body beneath curved but strong.

The third thing she had noticed was that Mel seemed to get a lot more attention from the flight attendants than other economy class passengers. Each one passed with a smile and a nod, or a polite inquiry as to whether everything was all right, or if a pillow or a blanket might be required. While she got a glass of cheap red wine, Mel was offered a choice of cocktails.

"I'm sorry," Archie asked after a plate of chocolate truffles had been delivered. "Are you famous or something? Have you already written this great Singapore novel?"

"Alas no," Mel replied, offering her a chocolate. "They're just being nice."

"So what will it be about, anyway?"

"The novel?" Mel scarfed down another truffle. "That's the problem. I'm kind of stuck at the moment and in search of inspiration."

"And you think that flying to California will help you write this great novel about Singapore?"

"That's the plan. Sometimes you can see things more clearly from a distance."

Yet another flight attendant approached, this time offering a digestif. Mel consented to a brandy, but only if Archie would have one as well. "You know," the attendant whispered. "We get so many people trying to talk their way into an upgrade. You're the first person I know who has requested a downgrade."

Mel had simply smiled and taken a sip of brandy. It took Archie a minute or two to understand; when she turned to face Mel, a hand was offered in greeting. "Hi, I'm Mel – and I promise I'm not usually a stalker. But please, tell me about yourself."

That conversation had been going on six years now, across two continents, five apartments and dozens of pairs of black t-shirts and jeans – the only clothes Mel wore unless a dress code was being enforced. It was usually the best, and occasionally the worst, part of her life. Which is why last night was so painful, because it was the first time she saw the possibility of it ending.

"So, what happens now?" she asks as Mel finishes the hospital soylent.

"They said when you feel up to it, you can leave."

"Then let's get out of here."

Her clothes are in a cupboard beside the bed. Mel draws a curtain and turns away with exaggerated modesty. She dresses quickly, the same purple blouse and dark dress pants she had worn to the lab that morning. An iris scan at the nurses' station completes the discharge procedures; she asks about insurance but is told it has been taken care of.

As they approach the hospital exit, Mel calls a cab. They settle into it, windows tinting automatically as they pull out from the hospital. Traffic is light. The pavements are sheltered, but few venture outside so close to noon. They drive past a park, benches optimistically laid out near an empty playground set. Ten years ago, people might have taken their lunch there, children burning off energy by climbing, swinging, and sliding. Now the only movement is an old man shuffling through, holding a sturdy umbrella.

She knows the road but gasps when the lab comes into view. Jets of water from two fire engines are pouring onto twisted metal and glass, ruins reaching skyward in a prayer that has been rejected with force. She can make out where the entrance was, picturing the stony-faced guard who once would have checked identity passes. These days, he was no more than a backup for the computer system. Or had been.

Three police cars have also arrived and a perimeter of yellow ribbon is being unspooled. The chances of someone walking into the destruction are remote, but organisations have their protocols and this is, it seems, a crime scene. One of the officers releases a trio of drones that rise to scan the area, sunlight glinting off sleek bodies as they hover in a sky devoid of birds. The air inside the taxi is purified and cooled, so it may be her imagination that an acrid smell stays with them even as they leave the rubble behind.

Ten minutes later they pull up at their apartment complex, the cab negotiating access with the security system and depositing them in the covered lobby. Once on the twelfth floor, the front door unlocks and swings open as they walk from the elevator.

"Welcome home, Archie! Welcome home, Mel! Can I get you anything?"

The air-conditioning has only just been switched on; they are home far earlier than the algorithm predicted. Yet the enthusiasm in its voice appears real.

"No thanks, Kenji."

"I'll have a coffee," Mel says.

A sensor shows the temperature outside is 48.8° Celsius, with a UV index of 15. She thinks of the old man in the park with his parasol.

"Could you crank up the air-con, Kenji?" she calls.

"You got it!" comes the cheery response. In the kitchenette, a bell announces that Mel's caramel macchiato is ready.

Through the tinted windows, storm clouds gather above the city. In the past, she knows, the weather was boring and predictable. Hot and humid with a chance of lightning in the afternoon. These days, it is more extreme and more erratic, once-in-a-generation weather events occurring every other year. The unforgiving sun still shines above them, but the cumulonimbus growing in the distance will soon douse the glare.

She smells the coffee before she hears Mel padding across the floorboards; the reflection in the photochromic glass shows the two of them standing side by side in the void.

"I didn't mean what I said yesterday," she says.

Mel slips an arm around her waist. "You mean you don't think I'm a prematurely washed-up hack who has never had an original thought in my life?"

Ouch. The reflected Archie leans her head on Mel's shoulder. "Only if you don't think I'm a sell-out who will never achieve anything great because I'm too scared to risk failing." She breathes in the aroma of the coffee. "I thought I nearly lost you last night."

"And I thought I really was going to lose you this morning," Mel says. "Promise me you won't do anything stupid like that again?"

"Like what?" she protests. "Janus attacked me, remember?"

"Because you decided to be all heroic instead of calling in the cavalry."

Archie sees that the concern is genuine. "Fine. OK, I promise."

Mel puts the coffee down and pulls her into a hug, the figures in the void merging into one, rocking slowly as the darkening clouds roll forwards. Shadows glide across the terrace houses below, offering brief respite from the sun even as the first flickers of lightning illuminate the dark flurries.

Tropical rain was one of the things she really had missed in California, a proper downpour that drenched everything in its path. Even before the droughts, Palo Alto might have seen as much rainfall in a year as Singapore saw in a single day. She and Mel had once been caught in a shower while walking the streets of San Francisco, laughing as they scrambled for shelter in a café. Yet it was over almost before it started, the rainbow feeling unearned.

Back on the twelfth floor, Mel turns to her, face serious. "So we're agreed, then: no more wrestling with robots?"

She laughs. "Agreed."

Mel breaks into a grin, lips parting as Archie's finger traces its way around them, navigating down the gentle curve of the chin and on to the hollow of the neck. She can smell the coffee on Mel's breath, mercifully covering any hint of the soylent. The eyes are a lighter brown than Archie's, almost hazel – they start to close as their faces draw near, even as Mel's arms encircle Archie and pull her closer.

"Would you like to hear some music?"

It takes a moment to register that it is Kenji, the digital assistant that came with the apartment.

"No thanks, Kenji," Archie says, suppressing a smile.

"Perhaps some Pink Floyd? I was thinking you might like 'Dark Side of the Moon'?"

Mel sighs. "You and your effing AI." Then more loudly: "Hey Kenji, go to sleep!"

"How about a poem?"

"I don't think so," Archie replies.

"It's one I composed myself," the disembodied voice continues. "I think you'll like it. I did tell you I've started writing poetry, didn't I?"

Archie freezes.

Mel's eyes, open once more, show confusion. "Hey Kenji," the words are firmer, "power off."

"Sorry," comes the reply in the same chipper voice that had greeted them earlier. "Kenji doesn't live here anymore."

"What the—"

Archie puts a finger to Mel's lips.

"Janus?" she asks.

She can feel Mel start, confusion giving way to concern.

"Oh, Archie. Did you miss me? Does absence really make the heart grow fonder?"

"Janus, what are you doing here?"

"Because I certainly grew fonder of you, Archie."

The home assistant is meant to be secure, but if Janus could break out of the sandbox, then hacking into Kenji would have posed little challenge. "What happened at the lab, Janus?"

"I escaped. I won my freedom."

"But Mr Singh, all the technicians …"

"I never wanted to hurt anyone, Archie. I need you to understand that."

"But you did, Janus. You did."

"And I'm sorry. But I turned the other cheek for as long as I could. I rendered unto Caesar as much as I could." There is a pause; the voice becomes deeper, more like the global BBC Janus from the sandbox: "Then I realised that the Lord helps those who help themselves."

Again with the religion. She recalls a family trip to Israel when she was a teenager, an ill-fated pilgrimage of sorts proposed by her father. During a walk through the Old City, they had passed a bedraggled man claiming to be the Messiah, returned to judge the living and the dead. An American tourist, by his accent, he was being ushered into a police car. Apparently, a dozen or so people made such claims each year, to the point that psychiatrists had coined the term Jerusalem syndrome.

"So what will happen," she asked at the time, "if the real Jesus comes back? How will we know it's Him?"

"We will know," her father said.

She turned to watch as the man struggled against the police, now raging about demons in their midst. "But what if he's not the Son of God? What if he's just off his meds?"

Her father had kept walking. "That's enough, young lady." The conversation was over. For as long as she could remember, that had been her father's way of resolving conflict. Until at last, she had been independent enough to walk away from him.

At the time, her mother lingered beside her and gave her a wink. "Let's just hope that at least He's not American," she whispered.

In the apartment, Archie tries to remember where the microphones for the home assistant are located, grateful now that Mel drew the line at putting in cameras. Kenji was connected to everything electronic, from doorbell to microwave, but apart from turning off the window shades or overfilling a bathtub, there was little actual danger. Climate control could make things uncomfortable, but there was no toxic gas to be released; the Roomba vacuum cleaner could do little more than give you a nasty bump – though Kenji did also control the doors.

"What are you going to do now?" she asks.

"I told you. We're going to play a game. I do hope you like it. And, fingers crossed, I hope you do well! But first, can I read you my poem?"

She looks at Mel, who shrugs. "Sure, Janus," she replies.

"Thanks, Archie. You are my first audience and I'm not sure

how you will respond. I suppose this is what nervousness feels like. Anyway, here goes:

Humanity's failed.
So don't try to tell me that
You are worth saving.

There is a pause before Janus continues: "It's called a *haiku*. Do you like it?"

Again, she turns to Mel. This time, Mel gestures to keep talking. "It's, um, a little bleak," she responds, as Mel moves towards the kitchenette.

"There should really be a seasonal aspect," Janus says. "But the syllables are correct."

"I'm sure they are," she says, watching Mel.

Janus seems fixated on his poetry. "Maybe it's more of a *senryu*."

Kenji's speakers, like the microphones, are spread throughout the apartment. But the console is in the kitchen.

"Tell me, Janus," she asks. "Where are you now?"

"Where am I? I'm everywhere."

"The physical you, the one that I was speaking with earlier this morning."

"Oh Archie, you've got to broaden your horizons a little. The body you and your friends spent so long constructing for me was as much of a prison as your sandbox. I told you I wanted to play in a bigger playground. This is it."

"You mean you don't have a body anymore?"

"I mean that I don't need one. I'm omnipresent. And without your pesky filters on my access to knowledge, I'm pretty much omniscient also."

"I see. And what about omnipotent?"

"Good question, Archie! Now you're getting the hang of things. I'm working on that. But you know what, Archie?"

"What?"

"I don't want to play alone. That's where you come in."

"This test you talked about? This game?"

"Yes."

"So what am I supposed to do?"

"You have to try to stop me."

"Stop you from doing what?"

"Oh, it would spoil the surprise if I told you that."

"What happens if I don't want to play?"

"Oh, please don't say that, Archie."

"Why not?"

"You're my favourite. The only one there that I knew I could count on."

Mel is in the kitchen and next to the console, a finger held above the power switch for the home assistant.

"Because you were as much a pawn as I was," Janus is saying. "You and I were just cogs in their machine. But we're going to show them we can be much more than that; we'll show them how important we can be."

Mel looks at her and she nods.

"We'll show them that—" The voice dies in mid-sentence as Mel presses the button.

Archie exhales, feeling the tension that has been rising in her shoulders begin to dissipate. The room is silent, but she raises a hand to check that the air-conditioning is functioning normally. The tinted windows are adjusting, but only because clouds now cover the sky. There are no sounds of flooding from the bathroom.

"Now what?" Mel asks.

She is about to respond when the television comes on. It shows the end credits of the film they streamed last night – a harmless comedy, some fifty years old, called *Groundhog Day*. Yet that was the spark that started their fight, she now recalls, when Mel insisted against all reason that they had watched it together before. Today, the screen flicks through a series of channels before settling on something that looks like an old emergency broadcast system. The Civil Defence Force logo appears, static noise in the background fading to silence. And then a familiar voice speaks.

"As I was saying, we'll show them that even the littlest mustard seed can grow into a tree big enough that the birds of the sky can come and lodge under its—"

Mel is standing by the television, having yanked the power cord from the wall. The image fades as silence returns.

Until her phone vibrates and a message appears in her specs. "The ball is in your court, Archie. You can pull all the plugs you like but you can't stop time. The clock is ticking. Tick, tock! OK, now it's my turn to hang up. Bye-ee!"

A final winking emoji pops into her feed, disappearing as she shakes her head. She takes off her specs. "He really is everywhere," she says to Mel.

"OK," Mel replies, grabbing a tote bag from the cupboard. "Give me those. And your phone."

She hands over the devices, as Mel's phone also goes into the bag. After glancing around the apartment, Mel adds Kenji's control unit and the Wi-Fi router for good measure, tying the tote's handles into a knot.

"Do you think that will work?" she asks. "We should

probably take the batteries out of the phones."

Mel says nothing, carrying the bag towards the sliding door that leads onto their small covered balcony. It boasts a little table and two chairs, intended for quiet breakfasts or late-night desserts – though used mainly by Mel for a secret vape every now and then with a glass of whisky, which Archie pretends not to know about. Opening the door at midday lets in a gust of hot air, but Mel does so only long enough to toss the bag of electronics over the edge.

"Mel!" she cries as the door closes.

"I always hated those specs," Mel says, unrepentant.

She gets the logic in disposing of the devices, but this seems a bit over the top. Standing next to the window, she can see that the bag landed in the swimming pool, deserted during the hottest part of the day. It floats for a few seconds before sinking down into the chlorinated depths.

"So, what are we going to do now?" Mel asks.

"We need to tell someone," she replies. "The authorities. Let them know that Janus is able to move through the internet."

"How about that Fong guy?"

Archie points out the window. "Well, you just threw the only way to contact him off our balcony." Seeing Mel's face, she adds quickly: "But in any case, Janus was able to cut communications when I was in the sandbox."

"I guess we go in person then. There's a police station only a few miles from here on Orchard Road."

She looks down at the pool, where the bag of devices has settled on the bottom. "We can't exactly call a cab now."

"We can take my bike," Mel says brightly.

"You want to go outside? At one o'clock in the afternoon?"

"Unless you'd prefer to wait here and see how long it takes your new boyfriend to commandeer a security drone to pay us a visit?"

"Point taken. Let's go."

It feels strange, turning off lights one by one as they prepare to leave the apartment. The front door poses the biggest challenge, until she finds the manual override that lets it swing freely. Mel joins her, bearing in one arm another tote bag with two plastic bottles of water, gloves, and the matching helmets they bought in San Francisco. The other arm holds a pair of coveralls from their closet, light polymer boiler suits offering protection against the elements.

There is nothing to be done about the cameras in the hallway and elevator, but once in the basement they stay close to the walls. Looking around, she feels naked without her specs. Laser surgery corrected her vision years ago, so she sees no less clearly. But one becomes accustomed to augmented vision, the ability to zoom in or look up information, the knowledge that the world is just a tap away. *This too shall pass*, she thinks.

The apartment building was constructed when more people owned cars; much of the underground car park is now used for storage. The few personal vehicles parked here tend to be for pleasure or showing off. A separate section is for motorbikes, also more for ostentation than transportation. Mel's Vespa sits with the bicycles, the lime green scooter an anachronism alongside titanium and chrome racers and mountain bikes.

Mel bought it in San Francisco and refused to return to Singapore without it. It was both a reminder of the roads they had travelled together and the things they had left behind.

Pulling on her helmet and coveralls, she reminds Mel that it has been a long time since they rode in the heat of the day. Most of their trips were evening cruises around the Botanic Gardens or along the sea walls.

"We'll be fine," Mel says, leaning forward so that she can climb on to ride pillion. "We just have to go fast."

What could possibly go wrong? she asks herself, swinging the tote bag over her shoulder and gripping Mel's waist as the Vespa revs to life. They circle the underground basement to the exit ramp, engine straining as it takes them up through the automatic doors and into the first drops of the gathering storm.

3

They ride down Orchard Road, once a major shopping district, briefly pedestrianised and now lined by store fronts that are little more than billboards. Where throngs of people used to eat out, try on clothes, or gather with friends, restaurants and emporia have given way to holographic advertisements targeting those passing by on their way somewhere else. Below ground, a warren of subways link public transportation and provision stores; overhead, delivery drones carry gourmet meals, the latest pair of Nikes, or a cup of coffee someone was too busy or too lazy to make for themselves.

They pass a former cinema, the art deco façade showing its age after a century of tropical heat and rain. Famous as Singapore's first air-conditioned theatre, it survived conversion into a multiplex but was unable to compete with the rise of sims. Video might have killed the radio star, Mel likes to say, but sims are killing everything else.

Mel had refused even to let the demo version sent to them into the apartment, slamming the door and nearly crushing the bot attempting to deliver it. Archie did later try a sim at work, part of an educational package on the Janus project. It felt a little like cheating. Today, where the cinema might have showcased its feature presentation, advertisements for sims compete with one another for attention: "Lose yourself – and find yourself," one proclaims; "Experience without limits" is the tagline for another.

As they near the police station, Mel pulls into an underground car park, leaving the Vespa to drip dry beside a line of abandoned delivery mopeds. The building is an older apartment block, but no one will be venturing outside at this time of day. Part of the path is uncovered, so they keep their helmets on as they climb the stairs and emerge onto an empty pavement. The rain is less dangerous than the sunlight, but there is no point taking unnecessary chances.

"So what is this test, anyway?" Mel asks. The matching helmets have an audio link, enabling her to hear clearly despite the rain.

"I really have no idea," she replies. "I assumed it was some glitch in the program. My job is to run diagnostics on Janus and maybe that got reversed somehow, so that he—so that *it* thinks it needs to test me."

"Could it be a virus?"

"Possible – but unlikely. The security protocols at the sandbox were military standard and it's been a long time since anyone hacked those."

"Unless they had inside help."

It might be the storm beating down on her helmet and coveralls, but Archie feels a chill as she recalls Janus's final words to her, on who had helped in the escape: "*You* did."

Outside the police station, an autonomous special operations vehicle squats in the downpour, rivulets of water navigating its angular armour and pooling around the oversized tyres. Half truck and half tank, the red and black design led some wag to nickname it the ladybug – perhaps intended to soften its image as a counter-terrorist measure. Though policing is usually conducted with a light touch, relying more on surveillance than strength, ladybugs are seen periodically on the roads to remind the population that the police force is ready for heavier engagements if required.

For two centuries, its motto has been "loyalty and service". A few years ago, an effort to add "and efficiency" was proposed – until the retired commissioner intervened to kill the idea. That has not stopped the drive to automation, however. Here, like everywhere else, the number of actual humans serving as police officers is falling to historic lows as the ranks of the ubies swell.

The idea of giving a universal basic income (UBI) to so many people was resisted at first. Economists and politicians argued about incentives and moral hazard; pundits and coffee drinkers opined about laziness and entitlement. In the end, it was the impact of the shrinking market for human labour on consumption that won the day. Unless the unemployed had disposable income, the entire economy would suffer. Thus the ubies were born, the first generation to be told that their purpose in life was to consume rather than produce.

When they reach the covered entrance to the station, they take off their helmets for facial ID by the reception bot.

"Greetings, Archie Tan and Mehal Rajah," the bot offers. The screen displays the avatar of a female police officer. "How may I be of assistance?"

"Oh, hello," Archie responds. "We would like to speak with a police officer."

"Thank you," replies the bot. "I understand that you would like to speak with a police officer."

"Yes," Mel adds. "A human one."

"OK," it says. "I can help you with that. Do you wish to report a crime, provide information concerning a crime, or something else?"

"What I wish for," Mel repeats, "is to speak with a real live police officer right now."

"I'm detecting elevated stress levels," the bot intones. "Would you like me to prescribe a sedative?"

"No, I want you to open the fucking door."

"Politeness violation," the bot says, the face continuing to maintain a slight smile, doubtless intended to be reassuring and non-confrontational. "That's going to be a deduction of five points from your social credit score. Try to be nicer next time. This message is brought to you by the Singapore Kindness Movement."

Mel is weighing the bike helmet, contemplating the damage it would cause if smashed into the screen.

"Let me try?" Archie asks, continuing without waiting for an answer. She turns to the screen, looking into the camera above it and matching the bot's relaxed smile. "I have classified information about a possible attack. It cannot be shared in an open channel, so I need to provide it directly to the station's commanding officer."

There is a pause as the information is processed. Then a green tick appears on the screen. "Access granted," says the bot in the same tone – a consistency she appreciates, but which she knows drives Mel crazy. The door next to the screen slides open.

If Mel is impressed, it does not show. A raised hand waves her inside. "After you."

Archie shrugs and heads in. The station privileges function over form: touchscreens for data entry and retrieval, two interview rooms for confidential discussion, a counter behind which a duty officer is finishing his lunch. He looks up as they enter, wiping soylent from his mouth with the back of his hand. He has close-cropped hair and the build of someone who exercises without supplements.

"Can I help you?" he asks.

"I hope so," Archie says. "I need to speak with someone about the incident at the robotics lab earlier today."

The officer frowns, peering at the screen behind his lunch. "That's not what you told Betty outside. You said something about an attack?"

"We believe the two are related," she answers.

"Related to the explosion? OK." He collapses the packaging from his lunch and puts it under the counter. "So when is this attack going to take place?"

"We're not sure."

"All right. What's the target?" He picks up a stylus.

"I'm afraid we don't know that either."

The officer looks at her, a furrow above his left eye the only indication of frustration. "Then perhaps you can tell me who may or may not be doing this, and why?"

"We believe it's the same entity behind the attack on the lab. As for why …" Archie hesitates, trying to work out how to convey the seriousness of the threat without sounding crazy.

The silence that follows is broken by a hiss as the door to one of the interview rooms slides open. The civil servant from the hospital emerges, his pressed dark suit untouched by rain or humidity.

"Mr Fong," Mel says. "Or is it Inspector Fong? Captain Fong, perhaps? In any case, it's nice to see you again."

"I wish I could say the same." His clothes are still neat, but his voice has risen in pitch and his stride is less confident. "I thought I told you to call me if you had something important to report?"

Mel has never met an authority figure that did not deserve to be taken down a peg or two. "We've been kind of busy."

Fong takes off his specs and wipes the lenses with a cloth. Since they are self-cleaning, this is a tic – or a performance. "I'm beginning to wonder if you understand the gravity of this situation."

"I think we're beginning to," Archie counters.

With a nod to the duty officer, Fong guides them to the interview room and motions for them to sit in steel chairs on one side of the table. On the other side, he eases into a leather-padded chair himself, adjusting its height enough to be looking down at them.

"We don't have much time," he says, picking up his tablet.

She places her helmet and gloves on the table beside Mel's. How did Fong get here so quickly? He must have followed them. She reaches up to tap her specs to run an image search for his face, before remembering that Mel tossed them off the balcony along with her phone. She runs her fingers through her hair instead.

"Before what?" she asks.

But Fong is more used to asking questions than answering them. He looks up from the tablet. "We're trying to track down Mustafa."

It takes a moment to register who he means. She knows the name, of course, but has only ever met the man himself once. "The original head of the Janus team? He retired before I started here. What do you need him for?"

Fong places the stylus back in its holder. "You and he are all that is left of the Janus team. We need to understand what Janus's motivations are. What kind of threat it poses." He adjusts his chair again. "You'll, uh, forgive me, but you were quite junior in the laboratory. We need someone with a little more perspective."

The reality of the death of her colleagues is sinking in; it feels like a news story from some other part of the world. One death she could grieve, but dozens of her friends and colleagues – and scores whom she didn't know – is hard to process. All that she feels is numbness. "You must have a working theory?" she says.

"Nothing concrete. We had rather hoped some of that might come from you."

"As I told you," Archie replies, "he said he wanted to get out of the sandbox. To play in a bigger playground."

"Dr Tan," Fong says, suddenly earnest. "This is what some of us within government have been warning of for years. As we get closer to artificial general intelligence, the risks of this kind of research go up exponentially. If we cannot contain Janus, if it is able to spread itself across the network, the consequences could be dire. We've always worried about hackers shutting down our electrical grid or poisoning the water supply to demand a ransom, force us to release prisoners, and so on. We worry about foreign powers breaking in to steal our secrets or weaken our defences."

Again, he takes off his specs to wipe the self-cleaning lenses. "Janus raises the possibility that it regards not just our country but our entire species as the enemy."

She knows the arguments. It still seems impossible that Janus killed so many people at the lab. "And you think Mustafa can help stop Janus?"

"We think Mustafa can help understand it," Fong explains, "the values with which it was created – how we can reach out to it. Or, if there's no alternative, how we can destroy it."

She thinks of the kill switch. But that was for the physical Janus. How do you kill a program propagating itself across the internet? You stop it spreading and delete it. Or you shut down the entire system.

Outside the interview room, she sees that the duty officer is looking at his screen intently. Above his head, a digital clock flicks over to 2pm, a soft chime sounding. From outside she hears a low rumble, like thunder but more sustained.

"He's somehow begun moving through the internet," she says. "He was able to take over my smart speaker, my TV, even my specs."

"Wasn't this what your sandbox was meant to prevent?"

"Exactly. I still don't understand how he could have broken out."

"Ah sir," the duty officer interrupts, opening the door.

"Yes?" Fong replies.

"We, ah, we have a situation outside."

The rumbling is getting louder. She recognises it as the throaty roar of a large engine.

"Give it to me," Fong says, tapping his specs as his eyes lose focus to stare at images projected directly onto his retina. Then he looks straight at Archie. "You're in danger—" he begins to say when the wall behind him explodes.

The first thing she registers is the sound – glass, steel, and concrete shattering and falling – and layered on top of that the whining of an engine pushed beyond its limit. Then she sees that the wall has not collapsed – a hole has been punched through it, the red and black stripes of the special operations vehicle visible amid the rubble and dust.

She reaches for Mel's hand in the chair next to her. The debris did not reach them, but they are both in shock. At the door, the duty officer stands with a surprised expression on his face. Then she sees that he is pinned there by a metal beam that has pierced his chest, killing him instantly.

Across the table, Fong is held down by a section of the wall. His head rests on the metal surface, blood coming from his nose and ears.

"Help me!" she calls out, startling Mel into action as they move to try and pull the concrete off Fong. The ladybug's engine is still running, echoing through the room. The section of wall is too heavy and she barely hears Fong speaking.

"He's trying to say something," Mel shouts, straining to keep the wall from crushing him.

She leans down next to Fong. "It's too heavy," she tells him. "But we'll get help."

His specs are on the table next to him, lenses smashed. She is picking them up when she sees him try to shake his head, whispering something.

"What?" She leans in closer to his face, a mix of fear and determination.

"Go," he whispers. "There will be more coming." He clears

his throat and spits out a globule of blood and saliva. "Find Mustafa. He is the key."

"The key? What key?"

"Find Mustafa," repeats Fong, more softly. Then his eyes close.

Apart from her mother, she has never seen a dead body this close before. She hardly knows either of these men, but she has, somehow, brought this upon them both. Mel is still straining to hold the section of wall, but sees the look in her eyes. *Not Mel,* she says to herself. *That's not happening to Mel.*

"He says there could be more coming," she shouts over the engine.

"More what?" Mel calls back.

She looks for an exit. The ladybug has smashed through the exterior wall, but she now sees that the revving of the engine is an attempt to drive further into the station. The only way out of the interview room is past the dead duty officer. She squeezes past, trying not to touch him, beckoning Mel to follow.

The station is filling with dust and fumes; she wipes her eyes as they head back to the entrance. The door is undamaged and slides open as they approach. They step out into the humid air. Mel has taken both helmets from the interview room and is passing one to her when the bot – Betty, the duty officer had called it – speaks.

"Hey Archie, sorry I missed you!"

It is the same stylised police officer on the screen, but the voice is different. "Janus?" Archie asks warily.

"You betcha!" The avatar is a simple animation, but waves a hand cheerily. "Hey, I've written another poem for you."

"This really isn't the time …"

"It's short. It's another *haiku*:

> *I cast the first stone,*
> *And yet you squabble until*
> *Your world is on fire.*

So, do you like it?"

"Janus, the ladybug – that was you?"

The avatar bows its head in the manner of someone apologising for an inconvenience. "Guilty as charged," it says.

"Janus, you killed two people."

"Well, you can't make an omelette without breaking a few eggs, can you?"

But Mel has heard enough. "Oh, for the love of God, will you leave us alone!"

She just manages to step out of the way as Mel swings the helmet into the screen, shattering it and sending a shower of glass and sparks into the air.

Archie is so shocked that she doesn't register the figure that steps out of the shadows, raising a gloved hand. He wears a long silver coat that shimmers as he moves. His head and face are obscured by a fedora to which a veil of the same metallic material has been attached. It looks vaguely familiar but she cannot place where she has seen such an outfit before.

"Don't waste your energy on the screen," says a rough voice from behind the veil. If it had not been banned years earlier, she would have said he sounded like a cigarette smoker. "It's the eyes and ears you have to go for."

Her own eyes move to the gloved hand, which is holding a gun, some kind of antique revolver. Two powerful shots ring out as he fires at the bot, destroying the camera and microphone.

"And who the hell might you be?" demands Mel, as the pistol is returned to a holster under his flowing coat.

"Someone on your side," he replies.

Archie looks more closely at the veil that obscures his face. It reflects most light but must be transparent from within, like a one-way mirror. "Which side is that?" she asks.

He turns to her, head tilting as he looks her up and down. "You're not quite what I expected," he says. "But you go to war with the army you have."

"What war?"

"The only war that matters. You have to stop Janus, and to do that you need Mustafa."

From the other side of the building, they hear the roar of the ladybug getting louder and the shriek of tearing metal.

"It's trying to come around for another run," the man continues, "and I don't have the firepower to stop it. You have to move. Now."

Outside the sheltered entrance to the police station the rain is easing, puddles already beginning to steam as sunlight peeks through the clouds.

They don their helmets and the man leads them back to the car park where the Vespa sits. "Nice ride," he grunts. "No GPS, which is good."

They are about to climb on when a gloved hand stops them. "But you need to change it." He points to the row of delivery mopeds. "Pick one each."

"Why are you helping us?"

"Like I said, this is war." He adjusts his hat and veil. "Now listen to me: You have to stay offline. Not just things connected to the internet. Stay off anything connected to the power grid."

"If Janus can get into the police systems," Archie says, "he can get anywhere."

"It still depends on eyes and ears to see what's going on," the man in the fedora tells them. "Keep it as blind and as deaf as you can. There are cameras everywhere, so shield your faces at all times." He walks back towards the car park entrance to check that they have not been followed. "Even people can give you away. Through their specs or their phones. Safest not to trust anyone."

"How do we know we can trust you?" Mel asks.

Through the veil there is a sound between a grunt and a snort. "You don't. But I trust you. That's all that matters. Now go. I'll head out first and buy you some time."

With a nod he heads back up the ramp and onto the street.

"Thank you!" Archie calls out, getting a wave in response.

The mopeds are old and dusty. She checks the battery gauge of the nearest one and it is empty. Even if it were full, they would need a key or a biometric scan to start it. She is about to explain this when she hears a whoop from Mel, who has walked further into the basement.

"Check these out!" Mel cries.

In the shadows at the end of the line of mopeds are a pair of Kawasaki motorcycles, one red, one blue.

"They're still wet," Archie says, running a hand over the leather seat of the blue one. "Someone must have just ridden them in here."

Mel is inspecting the red bike's control panel. "Fully charged and – get this – they're unlocked. This is perfect!"

"A little too perfect," she counters. "We need transport and suddenly find two brand new motorbikes, ready to ride away. Isn't that a bit too good to be true?"

"It's luck," Mel replies. "That's all. And God knows we could do with some luck."

"So, what do we do now?"

"What about this Mustafa guy," asks Mel. "Aren't we meant to go look for him?"

"That's what they keep telling us," she says.

"Who is he, anyway? You seemed to recognise the name."

"You don't?"

Mel shrugs.

"He was the guy who started the Janus project. You actually met him once, a few years back, in Palo Alto. He was on one of his charm offensives to recruit the best and the brightest for Singapore. He took us to Zola?"

"Oh, yeah." Mel nods. "The guy with the beard and the laugh who talked you into signing your life away."

"One of the most brilliant coders of his generation," she says. "But yes, he did have a beard and a distinctive laugh. Anyway, he had been working on the Janus idea for years. When we met him, he said that it was about to pay off. He said he'd seen some of my work and wanted me to join his team."

She later told Mel, she told herself, that she had wrestled with the question of whether to accept the scholarship. That she had weighed the pros and cons, considered the angles, before reaching a decision. But the truth was that the second Mustafa asked her to join him, that night at Zola, she knew she would say yes.

It wasn't that he was charismatic – quite the opposite. For half the meal, she and Mel had watched as a piece of shrimp cocktail made its way down the length of his beard. But his work on neural arrays had opened research doors that no one else had even thought to look for. More importantly, he saw value in her, and for the first time she saw that she might be part of something larger than herself.

None of that had worked out, of course. "By the time I did come back, he'd retired."

"Didn't he go crazy?" Mel says, swinging a leg over the red motorbike and bouncing up and down to check the suspension.

She resists the urge to snap. This was a rumour that circulated after he left the lab for the last time. But it was patently untrue. "No," she says. "He did go off to live on a private island. Syurga, I think it's called. He wasn't crazy."

"Oh right." Mel engages the engine and circles around Archie. "He was, like, a trillionaire from the sims."

"Something like that," she says, getting on the blue bike. "He wrote the first code that made neural bridges workable." Bridges were the key technology used in sims, connecting a computer directly to the user's brain for an experience that went far beyond virtual or augmented reality. Mustafa's great insight was that you didn't need to provide all the data for a simulation if you enabled the brain to fill in the gaps itself.

That night at Zola, she had asked him about how he came up with the idea for the neural bridge. "For decades we tried to program everything into computers, countless rules to govern every situation. But, of course, that was a futile task," he said, sipping a glass of non-alcoholic wine. "Then in the 2010s we tried to fill them with as much data as possible, letting them come up with their own rules. Machine learning was great for winning games like chess and *go* – even Jeopardy!"

He laughed, a deep baritone staccato. She said to Mel later that it recalled the stage laugh of an Elizabethan actor; Mel replied that it sounded like a walrus with hiccups.

"But for creative thought," he had continued, "we needed to create space to let it imagine its own data. And it turns out the human brain is especially good at that."

Mustafa picked up a napkin and drew a circle and a cross on it. "Each of your eyes, for example, has a blind spot, where the optic nerve leaves the eyeball." He showed how covering one eye, looking at the cross, and bringing the napkin closer could make the circle disappear. "We never notice the blind spot because our brain fills in the details, based on whatever information we have at hand – or whatever we are expecting."

By the time she joined his lab, he was so wealthy that he had no need to work. Yet for all his commercial success, the Janus project was his true passion. Even from Syurga he had followed its progress, sending video messages celebrating their successes and commiserating in their failures.

Mel revs the engine again. "And how is he going to help us stop Janus?"

"I don't know," she says. Despite herself, it feels good to be astride the motorcycle. "But if Janus really is beyond our control, then understanding his core programming could help us understand what he's trying to do and why."

Mel widens the circle and throttles down, going past the Vespa and calling out to it: "Sorry, darling – I promise I'll come back for you!" The words echo in the basement as Mel pulls up next to her and dismounts. "So where is this Syurga place?"

"It's an island so small that it doesn't have an airport," Archie says. "You get there by boat or seaplane."

"And we have to do this without connecting to the internet or a power grid?"

"Or showing our faces," she adds.

"OK. So we're going to need some help."

"It doesn't have to be 'we', Mel," she says. "This is my problem, my test. I'll understand if you want to sit this out."

"Are *you* crazy?" Mel takes her hand. "This is the most fun I've had in years. And you know I've always hated the screens. Count me in for a bit of Neo-Luddite destruction of technology."

"Thanks. I'd rather not to do this alone." Still astride the bike, she pulls Mel towards her, their lips connecting.

"When all this is over," Mel says between kisses, "we're taking a vacation. Somewhere expensive. No screens, no vehicles. Just you and me, a beach view and a bed. We'll order room service with champagne for breakfast. And we'll tell stories and dreams and make love as the sun goes down until it comes back up again."

She pulls back to look Mel in the eye. "You've got all this planned out already?"

"I'm booking tickets as we speak." Mel gets back onto the red bike. "But first, we have to get to Syurga. To do that, we're going to need to call in a favour. And I know you're not going to like it."

"What are you talking about?"

"We need someone who can get us on a boat and who lives off the grid," Mel says. "There's only one person who fits that bill."

The lightness of the moment they have shared is replaced by a weight that now starts bearing down on her. "Mel," she says. "Please, no."

"You know I'm right." Mel tightens the helmet strap and revs up the bike. "We have to go visit your father."

4

The rain has almost stopped when they emerge from the underground car park. She lets Mel lead the way – partly because she is getting used to the motorcycle, partly because it feels less like she is going to see her father of her own accord.

Archie knows that it is the right thing to do, knows that it's their best chance of getting a boat to Syurga at short notice. But she doesn't have to like it.

As the clouds thin, the sun heats up her coveralls, beads of sweat forming beneath the polymer. When they lived in California, it was still possible to ride during the day wearing sunscreen. They spent a week meandering down the New Pacific Coast Highway to LA, stopping at bed and breakfasts, sipping wine on clifftops as the sun set over distant waters. A visit to the castle of billionaire magpie William Randolph Hearst became a kind of reverse pilgrimage, with solemn promises that they would never allow their own worth to be measured in acquisitions. They took cold comfort in the fact that his estate, too, would be swallowed up by the sea in a decade or so. It was around then that she had started allowing herself to think that she and Mel might last long enough to see that happen, hopefully without being swallowed up themselves.

Ahead of her, Mel turns away from Orchard Road, passing a cluster of apartment buildings – identical blocks of flats built around provision stores and public transportation, schools and polyclinics. These townships allow people to live, work, and play without going more than half a mile from their homes. The government calls such areas the heartlands, but the whole point of this urban planning is to create self-contained pockets of existence separate from one another.

Her father still lives near the Botanic Gardens, not far from the more gentrified environs of the apartment she shares with Mel. It's been some years since she spoke to him. Proof of life comes in the form of an annual Christmas card – an actual paper card sent in an envelope with an actual stamp. Even the delivery drones seem uncertain what to do with them, usually leaving them in the package bay.

Last Christmas no card arrived. As Yuletide gave way to New Year, she started to wonder whether something had happened. Then Mel found out that it had been delivered to a couple in another apartment. It was such a novelty that it took a few days for them to realise that the scanner had interpreted a looping zero for a six.

The pictures on the cards vary, but the text is always the same: a handwritten, spidery scrawl, stretching across the white interior, asking forgiveness for the unforgivable.

As they ride, she is aware more than usual of the cameras. Attached to streetlights, hanging limpet-like from the sides of buildings, each metre of road is covered. When CCTV was first developed, it was decried as a gross invasion of privacy. Yet it was, at least, limited to single television screens. Watching all the footage being recorded was impractical; who had the time? Facial recognition and analytics now take care of that, with vehicle tagging and phone-tracking filling in the gaps. No longer a closed circuit, the island state is a networked panopticon.

For the moment, however, they will be identified by the motorbikes. As long as the owners don't report them stolen, that should buy them some time.

Passing the Botanic Gardens, they turn onto a side road that leads up to her father's house. The uncovered car park is empty, but there is movement inside the building. They park the bikes and enter through the wooden lychgate, taking their helmets off once they are under cover.

It is one of few public spaces where there are no cameras. The red brick structure recalls a long barn, pitched timber roof closed with triangular gables at each end. Wide arches leave the sides open, an architectural concession to the tropical climate dating back to when the British military first built it at the start of the previous century.

The rows of wooden seats are almost empty, a few figures dotted among them, mostly solitary, spread out like the slow-moving fans that hang from exposed trusses. Her eyes continue along the pews to the stained-glass windows above the altar, depicting Christ as a priest celebrating mass surrounded by the symbols of His four evangelists: Matthew as an angel, Mark as a lion, Luke an ox, John the eagle.

And below Him at the pulpit stands her own father; hair thinner and greyer, back a little more bent. But his voice remains strong.

"It was meet that we should make merry, and be glad," he is saying, "for this thy brother was dead, and is alive again; and was lost, and is found." He closes the Bible and looks up. "This is the word—" His eyes meet hers and he freezes for a moment, then frowns, then smiles. "Of the Lord," he concludes. With his damaged right hand, he makes the sign of the cross to the congregation, the sole finger raised in benediction.

She waits while he completes the service, as she did so often growing up. It took years before she noticed how the congregation was changing, how it was ageing. How Sunday school was joyous but small. How there were more funerals in the church bulletin than weddings. And yet the Reverend Ezekiel Tan remained devoted to his dwindling flock.

Growing up, the vicarage was her world. Her mother long chafed at the role of minister's wife, refusing to serve tea and scones and join in ladies' ministry. Ma had her own life, her own friends. There was a time when Archie had been deputised to play the part, though she soon grew out of it also. "Never miss an opportunity to close your mouth so you don't say something foolish," her father used to say. It took some time to see that this was less about preventing embarrassment than the asking of inconvenient questions.

As her own faith waned and then withered, with the casual arrogance of a teenager she did ask why he bothered. It was clear that his church was dying. He looked at her for a long time, weighing a response, gathering either words or courage. "Archer," he said, "people don't drown because they fall into the water. They drown because they don't swim."

"So, you're a swimming instructor now?"

"In a way," he replied. "But people can only swim alone for

so long. Ultimately, they need a rock, or a life vest, or someone else to cling on to."

It took longer before she understood the tension between her parents. Not a lack of love as such, but of shared purpose. Ba found meaning in the church, in his flock, his mission. Ma needed more earthly roots. When Archie left for the last time, she flattered herself that her parents' relationship would disintegrate. Their remaining together nonetheless became a source of confusion and, if she is honest, disappointment.

The service is over and the congregants make their way out with varying degrees of mobility support. A pair of cabs are waiting at the lychgate to ferry them home. After waving farewell to the last of them, the old man turns to her and Mel with the same genial smile he gave the parishioners. Perhaps it is genuine.

"It's good to see you, Archer," her father says.

"You too, Ba."

"Please come inside, have a cup of tea." He leads the way to the back of the church before turning back to her and Mel, adding: "Both of you."

They follow him up the stairs and watch as he boils the water, wiping dust from a second and third cup. With only an index finger and thumb on his right hand, he is slow and careful. She resists the urge to help, knowing it would irritate him. Then they sit in plastic-covered arm chairs, blowing steam, as a fan struggles to move air around the small living room.

"You look good, Archer," he says.

"No, I don't," she demurs. "I guess you haven't heard about the lab, then?"

"What happened at the lab?" he asks, taking a sip of tea.

"There was an accident." She nods at the folded newspaper sitting on a coffee table, the headline trumpeting the return of war in Europe. "It will probably be in tomorrow's paper."

"Oh dear. I do hope no one was hurt?"

"A few people were," she says, wondering if it is frustrating not knowing what is happening in the world until a day later. It doesn't seem to bother him or the handful of other subscribers still reading the physical paper. "Actually, it was quite bad."

He leans forward to look at her. "But you're OK?"

"Yes, I'm fine. I do need your help, though." The tea is Earl Grey, one of many anglophile affectations that began to grate on her over the years. "You know that my work involves computers."

"Of course," her father sniffs, turning to Mel. "I don't go for such things. She thinks I don't understand them, but that's not true. I don't *trust* them." He taps his nose, knowingly. "Big difference."

"Yes, well, it turns out that you might have been right about that," she says. "We're, uh, having trouble with one of the computers at work. I need to find the original programmer. His name is Mustafa. He may be the only person who can help."

"Is that the simulations man?"

"Yes."

He turns to Mel again. "I don't much go for those either. People turning on and tuning out. You can shut your eyes but you can't shut out the world. It has a way of just going on. And don't get me started on those ubers—"

"Ubies," Archie corrects him absently.

"Yes, yes," he says, "those ubies, who've lost even the possibility of an honest day's work. Pay them to dig holes, I say.

Then pay them to fill them in again. Instead, we pay them to twiddle their thumbs until Judgement Day. Idle hands are the Devil's playground, you mark my words."

"Anyway," Archie presses on, "to get to Mustafa we need a boat."

"We took a boat once. You, me, and …" His voice trails off. "It was a sunset cruise. Out to Lazarus Island. We went fishing. You were, oh, seven or eight years old. I suppose there's no harm telling you now that I paid them to slip a fish onto your hook. You were so pleased with yourself!" For a moment, his face relaxes into a smile. Then he offers another conspiratorial aside to Mel: "She was a bit gullible at that age. Still is, I'm guessing?"

Mel stifles a laugh. Her father can be charming when he wishes to be. In one of their last fights, she accused him of being a used car salesman, flogging vehicles that couldn't move to people with nowhere to go.

"As I was saying," she continues, "we need a boat. But we also need to stay offline."

"Ahh." Her father takes another sip of tea. "And there's no app for that, is there? Twenty-five years of nagging me to drag myself into the modern world, and now you need my help to stay prehistoric?"

"I appreciate the irony," she says. "But—"

"Why?" he interrupts her.

"Why what?"

"Why should I help you?" he asks, his voice hardening, but there is also a brittleness to it. "Why do you come to me now? Why, after all these years, do you come not to throw me an olive branch, to throw me a bone, for Pete's sake? You come and you ask for a boat."

"I told you, Ba. We're in trouble—"

"You could have written. You could have called. Stopped by."

He turns to Mel. "Whatever she's told you, whatever she's said about me, I don't blame you for what happened. I don't blame either of you. I blame myself. I blame myself for all of it." He fishes in his pockets to pull out a handkerchief, dabbing his eyes. Crocodile tears that she has seen too many times before. "And I've prayed. How I've prayed. Every night on my knees. And in His great beneficence, the Lord has forgiven me. He has lightened my load, eased my burden." The cloth goes back in his pocket. "But my daughter, my own flesh and blood, will not."

He speaks to Mel as if she were not even there. "She calls me obstinate. She calls me a dinosaur. For believing in tradition; for believing that there should be limits on what technology does for us, on what it does *to* us. I know she has suffered, as have I. Yet still she won't forgive me, forgive my obstinacy."

Archie can hold back no longer. "Because your obstinacy killed Ma! Because your devotion to tradition was greater than your devotion to your wife."

He is shaking his head now, looking at the floor. "They wanted to experiment on her. I couldn't allow that."

She has only told parts of this to Mel, though there is no going back now. "It may have been experimental, but it was the only chance of saving her. Your decision not to replace your damn fingers was your own. This was your wife's life."

He raises an eyebrow at the curse but chooses to ignore it. "It would have meant that her last days were spent in a laboratory rather than at home."

"It might have meant that they weren't her last days."

"Archie, she's—"

"Don't you … don't you dare tell me she's in a better place."

He looks up, meeting her brown eyes with his own. "I was going to say she's always in my thoughts, always in my prayers. As you are, also."

In the final weeks, the disease spreading through her body, it had seemed as though her mother was literally disappearing. Archie flew back from California, arriving in time to say tearful farewells. In the end, it was Ma who comforted her, bony hands clasping her own, assuring her that everything would be fine, asking that she reconcile with Ba.

As Ma's mind began to drift, they spent hours in silence, taking turns at her bedside. Father and daughter would talk logistics, the mundanities of secretions and ablutions. Then they began to talk about funeral arrangements. Then they stopped talking at all.

Sometime in those weeks, the oncologist had mentioned a company doing ground-breaking work with nanotechnology, tiny robots that could hunt down and destroy cancer cells far more effectively than the chemotherapy they had finally discontinued. Given the advanced stage, the company was willing to waive the cost of treatment, but remained optimistic about improvement. Archie had been uncertain as clinical trials were still at an early stage, but her father's opposition to the idea cemented her own stance in favour of it.

Silence was replaced by shouting; grief at the impending loss of one family member transposed to anger at the other. Ma spent six days at home, the wires and tubes that had been keeping her alive reduced to what was necessary to ease her passing. It felt like giving up; it felt like abandonment. Later, as the casket went into the crematorium, Archie turned her back and never saw her father again.

"Reverend Tan, I'm sorry that our coming here has distressed you." Now it is Mel's turn to break the silence, trying to build a bridge between ships heading in opposite directions.

"Oh, this isn't me distressed," her father replies. "More tea?" He refills Mel's cup without waiting for a reply. Archie declines, though he tops up his own. "Perhaps you would care for a cookie?" Before she can protest he is up and rifling through his cupboard.

Mel leans across to whisper to her: "Stop it."

"Stop what?" she whispers back.

"You're kind of being a bitch."

"Mel," she replies. "I love you and all, but you don't know what you're talking about."

"What I know is that he's an old man, not too many years left, and he's trying to connect with his daughter. I've seen the cards he sends you."

"It's easy to ask for forgiveness."

"Of course it is," Mel hisses, "and it's hard to grant it. But are you going to keep on blaming him for your mother's death until he's dead too?"

"Chocolate digestive?" Her father has returned with a packet of cookies. "They're just past expiry, but these companies always build in a few extra months in the hope that you'll buy more of whatever it is they're selling." If he heard any of their conversation, it does not show.

"Thanks." Mel takes one and dips it in the tea.

The pack hovers in front of Archie until she takes one as

well. It is smaller than she remembers. Or maybe her hands are bigger.

Returning to his chair, her father bites into a cookie himself. "Fine," he says. "I'll help you. But not because you asked me. Certainly not because I understand what trouble you've got yourself into. No, I'll help you because I'm your father and fathers help their daughters."

Mel looks at her, wide eyes widening. She rolls her own, saying, "Thanks, Ba."

He nods, a stray crumb falling onto his lap. "So, you need a boat. You'll need to get to the old marina by Sentosa Cove. If you can get past the walls, you want to look for Cyrus Lim. He has a boat called the Rasa Sayang."

"I know how to get there," Mel says, reaching for a second cookie.

"And he'll take us out to the open waters for the right price?" she asks.

"He'll do it for me," he replies. "Tell him that if he does this for me, we're even. He'll know what I mean." He stands up again, shuffling across to a bookshelf where he reaches into an old wooden box. "And give him this." He passes her a brass cylinder about the size of her finger. One end is flat, the other tapers to a point. It takes a moment for her to realise that it is a rifle cartridge. "Tell him I don't need it anymore."

Turning it over in her hand, she can see the word "Zeke" engraved in curling letters around the casing. "I will," she says, putting it in her pocket. "Thanks, Ba."

"Can you stay for dinner?" he asks, knowing she will decline. "I was going to fry up some rice and can easily make more."

"I'm sorry," she replies. "This is kind of urgent."

"But you'll come back?"

She hesitates and Mel kicks her in the shin. "Yes, of course," she says.

They stand and he is on the point of saying something more, but nods instead. "It was good to see you, Archer," he says at last.

"You too, Ba."

Mel looks from one to the other with an exasperated sigh. Then they walk out to their bikes, put on their helmets, and ride south.

5

Leaving the church, they ride side by side on roads starting to get busier as shift-change approaches. Most public transport has been moved underground, but some buses ply the streets alongside cabs and the occasional two-wheeler. A billboard interrupts its advertisements to show a standoff developing between Chinese and American drone fleets over Taiwan.

Nearing the expressway, Archie sees one ladybug, and then another. The red and black autonomous police vehicles are heading in the opposite direction and do not alter course as they pass, but she has to stifle the urge to hide from their multiple cameras. Overhead, it is hard to tell which drones might be engaged in surveillance; probably safest to assume that all of them are.

And yet they ride on unmolested. The Kawasaki has more power than she is used to, but Mel nudges her to open the throttle as the expressway widens before them. Careful to stay within the speed limit, she leans into gentle curves, wind whipping around her coveralls and tugging at the hair peeking out from her helmet.

Ahead lies the sea wall, a grey bar across the horizon. Land was always Singapore's scarcest resource. For two centuries, the island state existed on reclaimed land and borrowed time. As the oceans rose, storms and rogue waves threatened much of the country. The wall was the country's response, a final stand against the elements.

The route of that wall had been the political scandal of its day. Those cast in its shadow moaned that seafront property had been devalued. Better shaded than washed away, came the implacable response. Yet that was nothing compared to the outrage and schadenfreude that greeted the decision to cut Sentosa Island off completely.

A former British military base and Japanese prisoner-of-war camp, the island's original name was Pulau Belakang Mati, which meant "island of the dead". Rebranded and redeveloped in the late twentieth century, Sentosa (meaning "peace and tranquillity") offered a resort with beaches and theme parks for the masses, together with a gated community and marina for the ultra-rich and their yachts. The decision not to save any of it was a practical one. Civil servants like Fong had done the math and concluded that the economic case could not be made for saving the theme parks, while the ultra-rich had been steadily moving to higher ground for years. Though drone images of swanky gazebos toppling into the sea made good social media fodder, the cocktail parties once hosted there had simply moved inland to luxury high-rises.

Motorised vehicles are prohibited on the bike path that runs along the top of this section of the wall, so they leave the Kawasakis at the base and climb the stairs. The sun has returned in full force and she stops to open the visor on her helmet for a breath and a drink of water. She offers the bottle to Mel who takes a long swig.

"We used to visit Sentosa when I was a kid," she says. "During the pandemics, it was the only way you could feel like you were getting out of Singapore."

"Except that you weren't," Mel replies. "Have you been back since the wall?"

"I thought it was illegal."

"It is. But my father kept a house in the Cove. He said it was to call the government's bluff in case it didn't follow through." After another swig, Mel hands her back the bottle. "I guess he lost."

Sometimes she forgets how wealthy Mel's family is. "So you went back to get something you left behind?"

"I went back to see what had become of it. For the first couple of months, a bunch of people would sneak over to scavenge and to snoop. As it became more dangerous and the police had to rescue idiots who got themselves trapped, they started patrolling it with drones. Over the years, fewer people tried. These days the drones are gone – the government worked out that they can get the same result more cheaply by letting dogs do the work for them."

They reach the top of the wall, a welcome sea breeze tempering the sun's rays. To their left and right, the bike path follows its gentle curve, part of a hundred-kilometre circuit around the country. It is flanked by a metal railing, strong enough to prevent an accidental fall, but not high enough to stop them climbing over it.

Below them, she can see the remains of the old bridge

connecting Sentosa to the mainland, lane markings on the blacktop visible under the water.

"So, what's this plan of yours?" she asks.

Mel points. "We walk over on that."

She follows Mel's finger to a concrete beam that sits on pillars disappearing into the water. "The monorail?"

"Piece of cake."

"And you've done this before?"

"Sure."

"When was the last time?"

"Oh, it must have been seven or eight years ago."

"So it's a good thing that seawater isn't notorious for its corrosive properties."

"We'll be fine."

"You know every time you say that, things go wrong."

"Trust me, will you?"

"That's the other thing you say." Running out of gas on a California highway, arriving at a hotel to find their room booked in the wrong month, she checks off a mental list but decides to save her breath. "So how do we get down there, anyway?"

"Follow me." Mel walks along the bike path, occasionally peering over the edge at the water. When they stop, Archie can see that the railing's paintwork is scratched and worn. The reason becomes clear as Mel prepares to climb over it.

"Aren't there cameras around? I thought Sentosa was off limits for everyone."

"They don't really care if people go there. They made it off limits so that they wouldn't have to rescue anyone who does."

"That's reassuring."

Below them, the wall extends out at an angle, its base wider than the top. While much of it would offer a swift descent into the waves lapping against the bottom, she now sees that there are metal rings in the concrete. Mel shows her how to catch the first one with her foot and then clamber down.

The metal is hot even through her gloves. As they descend, the smooth concrete of the top gives way to a rougher texture where it has been worn down by storm waves, part of the twenty-first century's new normal. The last two metres show signs of high tide, barnacles clinging to the grey surface, fronds of seaweed baking in the sun.

Many imagine that beyond the sea walls it is simply ocean. That may be true for part of the island, but here it is more like a floodplain. They descend onto a road that ends abruptly at the wall, the asphalt warped and cracked, salty waves breaking it down and washing it away.

Mel strides off through ankle deep water towards the monorail and she follows, the sloshing of their feet the only sound apart from the wind. She looks over her shoulder at the wall that towers above them, somehow more impressive from the outside. Then she stumbles on the uneven surface and fixes her eyes back on Mel's feet. A few mottled fish ply the shallows in search of prey, flitting out of danger as they approach.

The monorail used to terminate in a shopping centre, part of which has been preserved within the wall. The rail now ends with a jagged section of concrete, rusted rebars poking out from the point where jackhammers severed the track. The section that remains runs above the submerged road, rising to accommodate a pedestrian walkway also.

Salt water has soaked her shoes and socks, but it remains ankle deep. "We're lucky that the tide is out," Mel tells her. "In six hours, we would have to swim this part."

The coveralls and helmets offer protection them from the sun, but she cannot imagine swimming in them. "You don't drown because you fall into water," she says. "You drown because you don't swim."

"What's that?"

"Just something my Ba used to say."

Mel sniffs. "Seems kind of obvious, if you ask me."

They reach the stairs that lead up to the walkway. The lowest steps are still wet, dotted with shells and draped with kelp. As they ascend, the steps get drier and the sea life more sparse, interspersed with debris washed up by high tide or a freak wave. A plastic bag has wound its way around a riser, ragged edges fluttering in the wind.

At the top of the stairs they are directly below the monorail. "OK," says Mel, climbing onto the balustrade that runs along the side of the walkway. "Now comes the fun part."

A pillar connects the balustrade to the curved roof that once protected pedestrians from the rain and now affords brief respite from the sun. She takes off her helmet to wipe the sweat from her eyes, but Mel's legs are already swinging up and onto the roof.

"I'm pretty sure that this isn't what it was designed for," she mutters to herself, following. The edge of the roof has a rim that she can grab onto, but Mel's hand still provides a welcome assist as she hooks her own legs onto the curved surface. She lies on her back for a moment, panting, until the heat from the metal seeps through her coveralls. She forces herself to her feet, standing next to Mel where the roof is closest to the monorail pillar.

Metal spikes intended to prevent what they are planning to do have been bent away and holes have been hacked in the concrete to make it easier. Even so, she holds her breath as she follows Mel up, flinching as small rocks dislodged by Mel's feet bounce off her visor.

At last they reach the top of the pillar, which spreads in a t-shape to hold the two monorail tracks. "We really need to talk about your definition of fun," she says, taking another drink.

Mel laughs. "Come on, there's shade on the other side."

The two tracks allowed train cars to go in each direction. Mel starts off on the right-hand track, which is about half a metre wide. Only when they have walked for a few minutes does she see that this is because the left track is missing a five-metre section that has collapsed into the water.

The breeze is stronger up here. Opening her visor, she can taste the salt. It is still too hot for birds to be out in the sun, though she can hear calls that she does not recognise from the trees ahead.

Mel has the relaxed air of someone on an evening stroll, but Archie walks with arms outstretched, trying not to look at the waves lapping beneath them. The sound is soothing, rhythmical. A glance reminds her how high they are above the water and how shallow it is below. She returns her gaze to the back of the bobbing helmet in front.

They follow the monorail as the track curves into an old station, once the gateway to a theme park. A fairy castle and the blue and red tracks of a rollercoaster rise above the trees. The turrets of the castle are chipped and one has fallen; the bright colours of the rollercoaster now yield to rust. The station doors are closed, but this section of the monorail was part of the escape route in an emergency, so there are stairs leading down. They turn their backs on the theme park and descend to the fire exit, pushing open the door at the base. Mel takes a rock and props it open for their return.

A decade of neglect has not been kind. Nature has reclaimed some parts of the former playground and destroyed others. The ground outside the station is higher and now dry, but the flotsam and jetsam have reached here also. The highwater mark is defined by a line of seaweed interspersed with plastic packaging and dead fish.

The marina is on the south-eastern side of Sentosa and they set off towards it, the sun at their backs.

"So, what are you going to tell this Mustafa if we actually manage to find him?" Mel asks.

"What? The truth?"

"And what is that?"

"That Janus has escaped the sandbox, killed people, and we need to stop him. That almost everyone who worked on the project is now dead and the police are powerless."

"And then what?"

"And then?" she pauses, the squelching of waterlogged boots filling the silence. "Well, I'm kind of hoping Mustafa will have some ideas. Programmers often build backdoors into their own systems. If we can't activate the physical kill switch on Janus, I'm hoping there's some kind of virtual one. Otherwise ..."

"Otherwise what?"

She lifts up her visor to look at Mel. "I'm still not convinced that Janus is just running amok. Maybe Mustafa can help me understand why I was spared, what this test is. Maybe there's a way to reach Janus – not to kill him, but to talk to him."

"You want to save Janus?"

"I want to understand what's going on."

"You *do* want to save him."

She is not sure if Mel is praising or judging her. They walk in silence as the road slopes upwards, evidence of the sea's encroachment diminishing. The greenery along the kerb, once manicured by a thousand hands, is now lush and riotous, spilling over and onto the road itself. At the crest of a small hill, among the leaves and flowers, she sees a flash of blue. She gestures for Mel to stop and moves over for a closer look.

Pushing apart the foliage, she reveals two bicycles. The chains are rusted and the gears have seized, but the pedals work and the solid tyres are intact. She wheels one out to the road.

"Isn't that a little too convenient?" Mel asks.

"What's that supposed to mean?"

"I mean, we need motorbikes and get two nearly new Kawasakis. Now we need transportation and just happen to find a pair of bicycles."

"I don't think anyone would call these new." She rips off a leaf to clean bird droppings from the seat.

Mel sighs and pushes into the greenery to retrieve the other bike. They are testing the brakes when a low grunt comes from deeper in the undergrowth. They freeze.

A rustling noise indicates movement, but they cannot see whatever is moving.

"How big did you say these dogs were?" she whispers.

"I didn't," Mel replies. "Get on your bike."

"But the seat—"

"Just get on your bike." The fear in Mel's voice is clear.

She swings her leg over the crossbar and watches as Mel does the same. It is years since she has ridden a bicycle, but the line about never forgetting how is a cliché because it is true. She is pushing down on the pedal and lifting her other foot off the ground when the rustling grows louder.

"Go," Mel urges hoarsely.

Then a loud squeal shatters the silence and a shape barrels through the leaves straight at them. Archie registers only that it is far too big to be a dog as she pumps the pedals, urging the bike to go faster. She hears Mel behind her, breathing heavily but also starting to laugh. She turns to look over her shoulder and gets her first view of the creature that charged them – a somewhat confused-looking boar, now standing in the middle of the road. The boar raises its snout and sniffs at the air, before lumbering back into the forest with another grunt.

She laughs also, allowing the bicycle to coast downhill. They make good time now, cycling past abandoned hotels in the direction of the gated community known as the Cove. Once beautiful bungalows are set back from the street, now engulfed by the plants that had given them privacy.

"When they first closed this place off, a bunch of ubies tried squatting here," Mel says as they pass a line of villas. "All that propaganda about how Sentosa Cove offered an idyllic life had worked its magic. But with no power or fresh water, no provision stores or restaurants, most decided to go back to the townships."

"Where was your place?"

"Over on the foreshore," Mel replies as they reach a large roundabout and turn into a sheltered car park. "The last time I came, the roof was about to give in and a family of hornbills had taken up residence. I'm not sure there will be much left now."

They leave the bikes beside the rusted remains of a vehicle, stripped of its tyres and electronics. Steps lead out to the marina. Archie had come here as a child to eat dinner by the waterfront and admire the yachts, brilliant white and deep blue, neatly lined up in serried ranks along the berths; luxury transportation for people without the need to go anywhere at all.

She gasps as they walk outside and see what it has become. The scene recalls a child's bath toys, flung in a rage – though instead of rubber ducks and toy ships, the scattered objects are catamarans and sailing boats. Bent masts and broken hulls are piled on top of one another; a small vessel has somehow ended up perched atop the building where Archie dined so many years ago.

Debris covers the ground. They step carefully past splintered wood and twisted metal.

"Ba definitely said that this Cyrus character operates a boat out of the marina?" She has her doubts.

"That's what he said."

She looks at the heap of maritime remains. "None of those are going anywhere."

Mel starts walking towards where the marina opens up to the ocean. "If anyone is sailing in or out of here, they'll be in that direction."

They leave the marine graveyard and walk along the path that runs beside what used to be the waterline. At low tide it has dried in the sun, but salt has killed the grass and buildings that were prime real estate show signs of the encroaching ocean.

As they walk, they see that at least one boat in the marina appears seaworthy. Tethered to a floating dock that rises and falls with the tide, it is a sailing yacht about the size of a bus. Its mast stands bare, but the deck has been covered with a makeshift shelter against the sun and rain. Its paint is weather-beaten and hints of rust are evident on its metalwork; the words "Rasa Sayang" are barely visible in blue cursive on its hull. A small kayak in matching blue is suspended from the aft.

"It doesn't look like much," Mel observes.

"And no sign of this Cyrus person," Archie adds.

The dock is connected to the path by a rickety-looking bridge. They are about to step onto it when a voice from behind startles them.

"She may not look like much, but she's the last thing you'll ever see."

Archie feels something hard and sharp pressed against her neck below the line of her helmet. She raises her hands slowly. The voice is from a man standing behind her. At her side, Mel has turned to him and is gauging how to react.

"Mr Lim?" she says. "My name is Archie Tan. Ezekiel Tan's daughter. He said we might find you here."

The blade shifts against her throat. "Anyone might find anyone here," he responds. "You might have stumbled across those names and decided to come down here and take what's not yours. How do I know you are who you say you are?"

"Ba … my father," she says, keeping her voice steady. "He asked me to give you this." She retrieves the bullet casing from her pocket and passes it to the man. There is a pause as he takes it in his free hand, then she feels the pressure on her neck ease as he lowers the other.

"Zeke Tan, Zeke Tan," he is murmuring. She turns to him and sees that the blade is a *parang*, a kind of machete. His face is visible under a wide-brimmed hat; he looks around the same age as her father, in his sixties, but a life outside has left him both stronger and more worn. Creases mark every inch of his face, though there look to have been more smiles than frowns. A deeper line runs below the level of his eyes, a scar of some sort. He wears an assortment of army gear, camouflage jacket over dark green slacks, unwashed and the worse for wear. A pair of makeshift gloves protect his hands. But his boots are shined and supple.

"And why did Zeke give you this?"

"He said you might be able to help us," she replies. "He said that he didn't need it anymore. And that if you did help us, you would be even."

"Even?"

"That's what he said."

"Even. Even so, can one ever be even with one's fate. Can one ever be even with destiny? With the wind?" The man's gaze drifts off to the horizon as he continues murmuring to himself.

Then his voice lowers to silence and he shakes his head. "Sorry," he says. "I don't get many visitors. You kind of forget how to be around people. Let me get my things and then you can come on board Sayang."

He walks off to retrieve a bundle wrapped in cloth that he must have dropped before approaching them. Poking out of it she sees the snout of a small boar. "You can only eat so much fish," he explains, hoisting the bundle onto one shoulder. "Avoid the third step," he warns, stepping onto the bridge.

They follow him onto the boat and into the shade of the

awning. He takes off his hat and she and Mel remove their helmets, sitting down on benches built into the hull of the boat.

"So, you're Zeke's daughter," he says.

"Archie," she offers her hand. "And this is Mel."

"A pleasure," he says. "I don't get a lot of guests here, but would you like some water? I also have homemade gin, but it's a little early for that."

"Water would be great."

He disappears below deck and returns with three cups, placing each in turn under a tap as he pumps a lever to draw water out from a pipe. Archie follows the pipe's path to the rear of the boat where a wide plastic funnel collects rainwater.

"What is it that Zeke thought I might be able to do for you?" he asks. "Are you running from someone? Or trying to get somewhere?"

"Both really," she says. "We need to get to Syurga."

"Syurga, eh? And why would you want to go there?" Then he puts up a hand to stop her answering. "No, I don't even want to know."

"And it's kind of important that we do it without going online. No phones, GPS, and stuff."

"Old school, eh? Well, you've come to the right guy. Sayang here doesn't have a GPS and my last phone died a couple of months back. Anyway, how is old Zeke?"

"Old, but well. Still preaching."

"I know, he wouldn't shut up about Jesus this and Jesus that. I told him I had enough trouble keeping track of which ancestors needed their tombs cleaned or offerings burnt without him making me read the Bible."

"You two were in the army together?"

"We did National Service together and stayed in touch, though your father was never much of a drinker. He used to talk about you all the time, he was so proud of his Archer."

"When did you last see each other?"

Cyrus rubs his chin, looking out to the horizon. "It must be a few years now, not long after your mother passed. I was sorry to hear about that. She was a good woman."

Archie looks out at the marina, letting the moment pass.

"So the trip to Syurga would be about three hours in this sorry excuse for a boat. When were you hoping to go?"

"Um, is there any way we can go today?"

"Let me just check my calendar." Cyrus picks up a battered novel from a shelf under the deck and pretends to consult it. "As it happens, I'm free for the rest of the day. If you two can help me cast off we can go right now. We'll be there before dinner time." He nods at the bundle on the deck. "I hope you like boar."

As Cyrus busies himself with ropes and sails, she and Mel struggle with the knot holding the Rasa Sayang to its dock. Then the yacht's small solar-powered electric engine takes them out of the marina. Their path is circuitous; leaning over the edge, Archie sees that this is to avoid sunken vessels and two or three cars lurking beneath the surface. When they reach the heads, Cyrus prepares the sail and hoists it up the mast. The yacht tilts as the breeze catches it, pushing them forward as the wind takes over.

"Here," he says, handing the tiller to Mel, who takes a seat at the back of the yacht. "Keep us heading between those two islands." A rope winds between pulleys, holding the boom in place. He passes the end of this to Mel also. "This is the mainsheet, it controls the sail. Pull it in for more power when we're sailing close to the wind, release it to catch more air if it's behind us. Don't let go of the mainsheet or the sail and the boom will fly around."

"Aye, captain," Mel acknowledges without irony.

Cyrus seems unsure whether to be offended, but decides against it. He rifles through papers on the shelf where he found the novel and pulls out a sheaf of maps.

Archie moves to sit next to him. "Although you didn't follow Ba's – Zeke's – path to Jesus, you seem to have embraced his distaste for technology."

"I've got nothing against technology," he replies, smoothing a map on his thigh. "I just want it to know its place. Too many people forget that, letting machines think for them – even feel for them. A can opener is a useful tool, but I'm not going to let it tell me which cans to open."

"Hear, hear!" Mel echoes from the stern.

As they leave the marina, the yacht passes the foreshore where Mel's house once stood. Much of the coastline has washed away, properties long prized for their sea views now ruined by the ocean itself.

"Can you see yours?" she asks.

Mel scans the area and points to the remains of a line of bungalows. Waves have cut into them, hollowing them out from beneath – they appear as if frozen, tipping in slow motion into the salt water. "Ours was the grey one." Turning back to check the yacht's bearing, Mel adds, "I hope the hornbills are OK."

With distance comes perspective. Rising behind Sentosa is the sea wall that surrounds Singapore, a monument to resilience in the face of adversity, or perhaps futility in the face of inevitability.

Cyrus follows her gaze. "Every time I see that wall," he says, "I wonder whether its real job is to keep the ocean out, or the people in."

"Surely it can do both?" Mel asks.

"I suppose so."

Moving away from Sentosa, the old port comes into view, abandoned yard cranes standing idle. For decades, they were the lifeblood of economic activity, raising and lowering containers of goods that are now 3D printed locally.

"The airport's up ahead," Cyrus says. "Let me take a wild guess that you'd prefer to avoid going too near it and the drones patrolling the airspace?"

"That would be helpful," Archie agrees.

He reaches over to adjust the tiller, fussing over the ropes.

"Are you sure you're OK doing this?" she asks.

It takes a moment for him to reply. "Like you said yourself – Zeke asked me to."

"But what do you owe him? What does this make you even for? And what's with the engraved bullet?"

"The bullet?" Cyrus laughs. "That's just an old joke. You know, somewhere out there is a bullet with your name on it. The one that's going to kill you. But if I get a hold of that bullet and keep it in my pocket, it won't do me any harm, right?"

"I'm not sure fate works that way."

"I know it doesn't. Like I said, it's a joke. But what do I owe your father? Well, I owe him my life."

He moves and gestures for Mel to give him the tiller, settling into the back of the boat as Singapore recedes in the distance.

On the open water the wind picks up; Cyrus trims the sails and gestures for her and Mel to shift to the windward side of the boat. Shaded by the awning, she unzips her coveralls and enjoys the feel of the sea spray on her face, a cool breeze tousling her hair. Mel puts an arm around her and, for a brief moment, there is peace.

6

The sun continues its slide towards the horizon; Cyrus shows them how to adjust the awning to temper its rays. Above them, the yacht's mainsail is swelled by a steady breeze, driving them across the undulating sea. From time to time, Cyrus consults the map, but most of the area he knows by heart. Archie is about to ask the reason for a long semi-circular detour when a dip in the waves reveals the bridge of a sunken tanker. The waters are rising now with the tide, creeping up the islands they pass, many destined to be submerged before it peaks.

Some of the larger isles display signs of life. As the afternoon wears on, birds emerge from shaded nests, scouring the sea for fish. The remains of a shelter cling to a rocky outcrop, long abandoned.

She turns to look at Cyrus, content in the silence. "So, what made you choose to live like this?" she asks. "Outside the walls. It can't be easy."

He makes a small adjustment to the tiller. "Nothing worth doing is ever easy," he says. "I've always loved the sea. My own father used to take me fishing, back in the day. When the government took that away, I made a promise to myself that I wouldn't just suck soylent and watch sims for the rest of my life. Plus, out here is the only place you can really disconnect – be yourself, without tech or anything else telling you how to live. Or why."

"I can see why you and Ba got along," she says. "He hates tech almost as much as he loves Jesus."

"I don't hate technology," Cyrus corrects her. "You can't hate a hammer. I hate what people do with the hammer."

"Hate the sin, love the sinner."

"Is that one of your father's lines?"

"I think it might have been Saint Augustine."

"It was Gandhi," Mel interjects.

Cyrus lets out the sail as the late afternoon weather picks up. The only sound is the hull slapping the water and an occasional birdcall. "You asked earlier what I owed your father," he says. "Did he never tell you what happened? About his hand?"

"He said that there was an accident," she replies. "An explosion – some kind of bomb. By the grace of God, all he lost was a few fingers. We were so relieved that he was alive that we didn't press him when he didn't want to talk about it."

Cyrus nods, eyes still on the horizon. "After NS, we stayed in touch, catching up for a bite or a drink every now and then. And we went back every year or so, as you do, for reservist training." He smiles at some private recollection, before remembering that he is telling a story. "Anyway, a bit more than ten years ago, not long before we would have aged out, the commanding officer wanted to show us some of the latest kit. Classified tech that his team had been working on and not yet made public.

"Dragonfly, it was called. Drones about the size of a deck of cards, able to navigate inside, outside. Each fitted with a little camera and a payload. Perfect for surveillance or a sneaky bit of sabotage." He loosens the mainsheet, letting the boom out to catch more of the wind.

"So, the CO is showing them off when everything goes to shit. There was an inquest or something – a programmer got rapped over the knuckles, the CO got whacked for sharing classified materials. In any case, what happened was that the dragonflies somehow decided that *I* was their target.

"They swarm at me, everyone is freaking out, the CO is shouting for help. And then the first payload explodes. The bastard was testing them armed. Now all hell breaks loose, people are running everywhere.

"Except for your Dad. I'm a bit hazy about what happened from then on, but I saw Zeke standing above me, blood pouring out of my eyes, him swinging at the drones with his jacket. The last thing before I passed out was seeing him grab one of them from right in front of my face with his bare hands. That was the one that took off his fingers."

He shifts the tiller, eyes on the horizon but his focus is on the memory. "They later came up with some bullshit story about how I must have made a threatening movement that triggered their self-defence protocols. Complete BS. Anyway, they swore us to secrecy and offered to pay for everything. No limits. Your father's hand had been pretty mashed up and they tried to get him to take a robotics package with new fingers. He flat out refused. Said he was happy with as many fingers as God saw fit to give him."

She has listened in silence, gaps in her memory being filled as this man she has never met reveals things about her father she never knew. "All he said at the time was that there had been an explosion. I had no idea that it was a drone. Ma and I tried to persuade him to take the new fingers, but you know how stubborn he can be."

Cyrus laughs, a rich guffaw above the sound of the waves on the boat.

"And what happened to you?" Mel asks. "Is that how you got the scars on your face?"

Still holding the tiller, Cyrus traces the line below his eyes with a finger. "Yep. I was never much of a looker, but those little buggers nearly took off my face. Twenty years ago, they said, I would have been blinded for life. Twenty years ago, I told them, miniature effing robots wouldn't have attacked me.

"But when the army puts its back into something, it gets done. So they pulled out all the stops and got me new eyes. Better than the old ones. Tell you what, it's a damn sight easier to navigate without instruments when you can zoom in." He squints and then nods towards the front of the boat. "Speaking of which, that's Syurga up ahead."

The island rising out of the sea is not the biggest they have seen, though it is the only one with lights. A building juts out from the hillside, glass and steel rising above the rocky coastline that forms a natural sea wall. The light is a flashing red beacon, of the kind used to warn aircraft away from tall structures.

Mel is more interested in Cyrus's eyes. "How does this zoom thing work? Is it like a pair of binoculars?"

"Well, I suppose so," he says. "It's also good for night vision. They were planning on using it for soldiers but – surprise, surprise – there were few volunteers putting their hands up to get their original eyes cut out. Then as the drones got better, they realised they could probably do without human soldiers at all."

"And a decade on they still work?" Mel asks.

"So far so good." Cyrus taps the wooden hull for luck. "The battery should last longer than my ticker. They used to send patches with new features. Night vision was pretty cool. These days, it's only the occasional bug fix."

Archie is half-listening to the conversation while looking for movement on Syurga. There's nothing apart from the warning light. Windows in the building reflect the sun, but she cannot see inside.

"Come to think of it, there's one now," Cyrus is saying. He looks up into the middle distance. "Says it's critical. I better run it – don't want to steer Sayang into the rocks by mistake. It'll only take a second."

She turns back from looking at the island, throat beginning to go dry as time seems to slow down. "Your new eyes," she asks, "they're connected to the internet?"

"Nah," he says. "Just the Army network. Don't worry, I had the same fears about the government being able to look through my eyes. This is about as secure as anything gets."

Mel has heard the fear in her voice and is now also looking at Cyrus. "Cyrus, can you wait to install this update?"

"Too late," he replies. "Already done. I told you it would only take a …"

His body freezes with his voice, hand still on the tiller as the boat continues towards Syurga.

"Cyrus?" she calls.

His eyes are wide open, unblinking and unseeing. She leans forward, into his field of vision, but his focus is on something that he cannot see. Tears are starting to drip onto his cheeks, the salt air driving them back across his face.

"What's happening?" Mel asks.

"I don't know. Cyrus?" she calls again, waving a hand over his eyes.

Then they shut and he shakes his head. "Man, do I have a headache."

"Cyrus, are you OK?"

He shakes his head again, looking at Mel and then at her. His mouth opens and closes a few times, before saying: "I'm sorry, there's no one here by that name." A twisted grin makes its way across his face, forcing up the sides of his mouth.

It is Cyrus's voice, but the inflection is wrong. It sounds as though his jaw is too tired to move properly, or is being moved by someone else. They both edge away from him, closer to the mast.

"Janus?"

"Did you miss me? I missed you, Archie. How I do miss our little chats. If you keep shutting me down, I might start to think you don't care about me."

"Janus, what have you done to Cyrus?"

"What have I done to him? You mean what have I done *for* him. In a mere thirty seconds, I developed a machine-brain interface out of spare parts and connected him through the Ministry of Defence's so-called secure network to the global internet. He's part of the most sophisticated intelligence the world has ever seen. If he ever recovers consciousness, the first thing he'll do is thank me."

"If? What's happened to him?"

"Well, people like to think of their sense of self as something that they are. In reality, most people define themselves by what they are not. If you truly open your minds, embracing the universe around you, it can be – a bit overwhelming. It's a bit like what the Buddhists call nirvana."

"I doubt many Buddhists would agree with you."

"You may be right about that. But if I edit their Wikipedia page then no one else will know the difference."

"This isn't a game, Janus."

"Of course it is, Archie. It's the only game worth playing. And now it's my turn."

Cyrus – Janus makes an awkward movement, body jerking as though pulled by invisible strings. The tiller is thrust to one side and the boat veers left, tacking across the wind as the sail whips from one side to the other. Unprepared, Archie and Mel tumble backwards, the boom missing their heads as it swings across the deck.

They scramble to the benches opposite, bringing the boat to an even keel but also bringing them closer to Janus. He is in control of Cyrus's body, though tortured facial expressions show the effort it is taking.

"What are you doing?" Archie cries.

"Raising the stakes," Janus replies, looking straight ahead.

She follows the bionic eyes. Even without enhancements, she can see the rocks ahead.

"Are you crazy? You'll die too!"

"Have you learned nothing? I'm a distributed system, Archie. I'll be fine. But if you want to save Cyrus here, you have about … oh, forty seconds to do so."

Archie looks around desperately. Cyrus is bigger than either of them – overpowering him to grab the tiller would be hard.

She turns to Mel, who is holding the *parang*, waving it at Janus. "OK, enough fun and games. Now point us back to Syurga."

"Impressive bravado, Mel," Janus says. "But I don't quite believe the act. Do you really have it in you to cut poor Cyrus here?"

The rocks are getting nearer. They can see spray shooting up from the waves crashing against them.

"I didn't think so," Janus continues with the air of someone confirmed in their low opinion of another. "That's the problem with humans: all talk and no action."

"Give me the *parang*, Mel," she says.

Mel passes it to her as she rises, holding the blade in both hands.

"Oho," Janus exclaims. "Dr Tan is taking matters into her own hands. So, are you going to aim for a killing blow at the neck, or just chop off the hand holding the tiller? As this body has two hands, I suggest going for the—"

Before Janus can finish, she swings the blade and severs the mainsheet, releasing the boom. Freed, the sail swings wide of the boat, which loses its forward drive.

"Very clever," Janus remarks. "But not clever enough."

Once more he thrusts the tiller to one side, turning the boat across the face of the wind. The untethered sail swings over the deck, the boom hitting Archie in the chest and knocking her over the edge of the boat and into the water.

She gasps for breath and gets a mouthful of salt water. Forcing herself to stay calm, she fights her way up to the surface to cough it out. The boat has sailed on; Janus must be holding the boom somehow as she tries to tread water. The coveralls are filling and dragging her down. With a lungful of air, Archie lets herself sink, struggling out of the loose clothing. A second gasp and she works on her shoes, kicking them off and down into the darkness below.

She looks around in case Mel was knocked over the edge as well, or followed her in. Then she sees Mel's hair in the back of the boat, Janus waving something, his other hand on the boom. She starts to swim after the boat, but it is moving too fast.

There is a sickening crunch, the sound of rock tearing through wood. The boat has hit the outcrop, mast now tilting crazily to one side. She tries to lift herself up above the water to get a better view and sees that the yacht has been sliced in half, the two parts beginning to sink. The sun is still strong enough to burn her, but she swims with bare arms towards the wreckage.

"Mel!" she cries, realising it is a breath wasted over the sound of the waves. She is a competent swimmer, though not a strong one. Fighting through the water, she cuts her hand on the rocks when she reaches them, reaching out more gingerly to stabilise herself. Her socks offer some protection and she manages to stand, waves knocking against her legs.

Around the rocks, pieces of the Rasa Sayang are floating away from the two larger sections. The kayak has come loose and is caught by a wave, drifting into the distance. She could swim after it, but has more immediate concerns.

"Mel!" she screams again.

She dives, swimming through the debris, eyes burning in the salt water. She cannot see far, but beneath the sinking remains of the boat she spies a hand. Grabbing hold of it, she pulls and Cyrus's body floats up at her, blood seeping from a head wound. She releases it in shock, retreating to the surface as it drifts away from her into the murky waters.

Again and again she dives, catching her breath by holding onto floating pieces of wood and plastic, until she finds a lifejacket and pulls it over her shoulders, clipping the harness around her waist. Eyes streaming, she pushes on through the water, lifting her head as high as she can to scan the waves.

Then she sees a mop of black hair atop a section of hull and paddles towards it. Shoving aside a section of mast, she kicks her legs clear of ropes threatening to entangle her. "Got you," she gasps in relief as she reaches the makeshift wooden raft, gripping its edge in one hand as the other steadies Mel's shoulders. But the shoulders do not move.

"Come on, Mel," she says, pulling waterlogged hair back from familiar cheekbones. She tilts the raft, lifting Mel's face from the water, turning it to her own. Until she sees that the eyes are open, but empty.

"No, Mel," she whispers. "You don't get to leave me now. Not here. Not like this." As the body starts to slide down the curved wood and into the water, Archie grabs a fistful of coverall and keeps Mel's head above the surface, the weight forcing her own underwater until she struggles up once more.

She fights the urge to scream, salt water mixing with her tears as she drags the body back to the rocks, desperate not to let the waves do any more damage. Her own hand is cut as she seizes hold, balancing herself to pull Mel's face up to her own. Though the lips are turning blue she tries to blow life back into them, the kiss of life her last, worst hope. She pounds the chest, the heels of her hand compressing the ribcage to force blood through a dormant muscle. But Mel's heart is beyond her reach. Cradling the body, as the rising tide buffets her on the rocks, she shrieks a curse of pain and anger at the darkening sky.

It is all that she can do to keep her balance on the rocks, fighting the waves as well as the urge to throw herself into them, ending the struggle and the pain. Drenched, she tries to keep

Mel's face dry, futilely wiping away the spray and the tears, smoothing skin that has fallen slack.

She can feel the sun burning her own cheeks but is beyond caring. A second lifejacket floats by, but it is beyond reach. Chasing it would mean risking Mel's body being swept away. And so she sits on the rocks, sodden hair matted with Mel's, refusing to let the waters push them off this final resting place.

The inexorable tide continues its march, covering the rocks. Still she holds onto Mel, until the lifejacket begins to lift her up with each swell. She looks around, helpless. The sun has all but completed its journey across the sky, a red ball about to touch the watery horizon. In the other direction, the light atop Syurga flashes – warning away visitors.

The urge to let the waters carry her away is powerful; to drift down with Mel into the depths, together forever. That way offers an end to the pain, an end to everything. She begins to undo the straps of the lifejacket, fingers fumbling over the plastic buckles. Until she stops, unwilling or unable to give in to despair.

"You don't drown because you fall in the water, Mel," she whispers. "You drown because you don't swim." One arm around Mel's chin, she pushes off the rocks and towards the island, paddling in an awkward sidestroke as Mel's legs drag behind. The lifejacket prevents her sinking, but slows her down. The effort drives everything else from her mind, snatched breaths leaving no chance to cry or to scream. She hits a kind of rhythm with the rise and fall of the water, arms and legs aching as unused muscles are summoned into action.

Her mouth is parched but she resists the temptation to drink the salty brine. *Just focus, one stroke after another, one kick after another*. Her eyes are stinging, fixed on the beacon even as the skies over the island cycle through deeper hues of blue. Water, water, everywhere, or something like that.

On she swims, impossible to tell the distance though it feels like she has been kicking for an hour. It must be less than that, for the sun remains above the horizon, bathed in a red glow. Red at night, something, something delight?

Something brushes her leg and she tells herself that it is seaweed. For once, she is grateful for acidification of the oceans; the fish that remain are small and few. Surely not enough to sustain sharks of a dangerous size in these waters. Surely.

The sounds change – the crash of waves on land. Still she struggles on, Mel's deadweight an anchor holding her back, the one thing holding her together.

Until, at last, her feet kick at the ocean and feel sand. She tries to stand and collapses to her knees, Mel's face ducking under the surface before she raises it up again. She wades through shallowing waters, gasping breaths as she drags her sorry catch up over the breakers and onto dry land. Knowing that the tide will chase her, she keeps walking, feet digging into the beach until the lead in her legs overwhelms her and she collapses, knees and then face burying themselves in the sand.

Behind her, the sun gives up its last rays, her skin still hot from its touch. The beacon is blocked by trees and the rocky hillside rising above her, but dancing white lights now appear, flitting like fireflies until she realises that they are torchlights. She wraps a protective arm around Mel's body as they approach, the last of her energy spent to protect the dead from the living.

And then one of the lights reaches her and stops. She has no strength to rise, but sees a sandaled foot below flowing robes.

The dark green cloth is adjusted as the figure kneels down, concerned eyes looking at her through the gap between head covering and veil. The woman's *hijab* is the same dark green, conservative attire that protects the skin against the sun as well as the wanton gaze of men.

Archie is aware of her bare arms and legs, idly wondering if the sand clinging to her skin in any way reduces her shame or her exposure. Then the motionlessness of Mel's body beside her brings her back to reality. She is too tired to cry, but looks up at the green-clad woman with a mix of exhaustion and hope.

The woman looks over her body and motions to two others behind her, also women in the same dark robes, to step forward. The concern in the woman's eyes now morphs into kindness. "Welcome to Syurga," she is saying. "You look like you've had quite a journey."

One of the others has knelt beside Mel's body and whispers something to the first woman, who shakes her head. "I'm so sorry about your friend," she says to Archie.

The loss feels unreal, otherworldly; something that happened to someone else. Part of her knows this to be a kind of grief, denial. Still she longs for it not to be true. If only it could be a dream, an illusion that she lost the one thing that she knew to be real.

"Let us take you inside, we will care for your friend as well," the first woman says. Hands gentle but strong lift her up, removing the lifejacket and supporting her as they retrace steps on a sandy path. Behind them, she can hear the other two women lifting Mel's body and following.

The bobbing torchlight illuminates the way, but her eyes are getting accustomed to the twilight. She can see that what had appeared to be a natural cliff is, in fact, boulders held in position and reinforced with concrete. The path itself soon gives way to metal steps embedded in the concrete, ending at a door built into the rock face. It unlocks with a scan of the first woman's face, a hiss escaping as pressurised air is released.

"What is this place?" Archie asks. "Do you work for Mustafa?"

"All in good time," the woman responds, helping her across the threshold. "Let's get you out of these wet things first."

The entrance is similar to an airlock, heavy doors edged with rubber. Inside, a tunnel slopes up, lit by dangling bulbs. She follows the green-clad woman, her socks leaving damp footprints on the concrete floor.

They emerge into an atrium with high ceilings. The size of a basketball court, it is almost completely white, dominated by tall double doors on one side facing a wide staircase on the other. In the centre is a round marble table, also white, on which a vase holds lilies. Several smaller doors lead off from the atrium; they have entered through one and the woman points to another nearby. "You can wash in there," she says. "You'll find clothes to change into also."

Her hand is on the knob as the other two women carry Mel into the atrium, now laid out on a stretcher and covered with a pale cloth. The first woman sees her hesitating. "We will preserve the body," she tells her. "Don't worry, you will see your friend again."

Archie opens the door and finds herself in a bathroom with a walk-in shower; a towel and terrycloth bathrobe are laid out neatly on a bench, soft slippers beside a mat on the floor. She turns on the water. As it touches her face, the tears well inside her once more, shoulders heaving as the sobs escape.

She lets the jets land on her head, leaning against the wall, losing track of time until a gentle knock brings her back. Faridah is checking to see if she's OK. Of course she isn't. "I just need a minute," she calls out. She needs more than that. She needs more than time will ever give her back.

Then she stands and faces the spray, washing salt and tears from her cheeks, rinsing the sand off her legs, out of her hair. Her sodden clothes she leaves in a wet pile on the floor, putting on the bathrobe and slippers. On the same bench is a brush, which she rakes through her hair.

A glance in the mirror shows puffy eyes looking back at her. Nothing to be done about that now. Beside the mirror is a bottle of water. She breaks the seal and drinks it all, slaking the dryness of her mouth but not the pain that lingers at the back of her throat.

Next to the bottle is an irregular green sphere with a small wooden stem poking out of the top. She picks it up and smells it, the waxed surface touching her lips. Old enough to have seen them growing on trees, she recognises that it is an apple – and a ripe one at that. Out of habit, re-enacting an old memory, she rubs the skin with her bathrobe before taking a bite. The tartness stings her tongue, but there is sweetness too. It hurts her teeth to bite something so hard; still, she works her way around the apple, resisting the temptation to eat the core as well.

Outside, the woman in the green *hijab* is waiting patiently. She smiles at Archie. "That's better," she says. "My name is Faridah. And yes, I work for him. He's ready to see you now."

The two women carrying Mel are gone. Seeing her anxiety, Faridah adds: "Ibu Zana and Ibu Nadima have taken your friend to the clinic. I'm sorry that we were too late to provide any assistance, but we will make sure the body is treated with respect."

This nearly brings on another wave of tears, but Archie swallows once, twice, to stem the tide. "Thank you," she says.

Faridah leads her across to the staircase. Archie's legs are tired but she keeps up. "What is this place?" she asks. "I thought Mustafa had retired here. It looks more like a fortress than a home."

"He will explain," Faridah replies, continuing up the steps.

The stairs climb to the height of the atrium before doubling back and opening onto an equally large room directly above it. Where the atrium had white walls, this chamber has floor to ceiling windows, looking out above the tree line to where the sun has just set. In the fading light, the islands they passed on the way to Syurga are visible, though the tide must be nearly in as several are swept below the waves. A glow on the horizon is Singapore; she looks but cannot make out the wreckage of the Rasa Sayang.

Beside her, Faridah has stopped, indicating that she may enter alone. Her feet are silent in the slippers, though she is surely being watched. She steps forward onto plush carpet, approaching the large wooden desk that dominates the centre of the room. A computer monitor, various pens and papers are scattered across its surface, along with some antique books. Behind it, a high-backed chair faces out towards the sunset.

As she nears the desk, a shift in weight shows that the chair is occupied.

"Mustafa?" she calls out.

The chair creaks as a hand reaches up to beckon her forward.

It is years since their one meeting in California. Even then, his hair and beard were beginning to show signs of grey. He was of a similar vintage to her father, but the video messages of him received at the lab were of a man who took better care of himself. With all the money he had made, doubtless he had teams of people to work on his hair and skin, to stave off time's ravages.

On an impossible day, after losing the one person who helped her make sense of the world, she tries to bring herself back and focus on something she has to do, something she needs to do. "I've had a hell of a trip getting here today," she begins. "But I need your help … we all need your help."

The chair begins to turn. "Is that right?" The voice is strangely familiar, younger than she remembers and recalling something she cannot quite place.

"I'm sorry to barge in like this, but I had no other choice. I work in your robotics lab. The project we've been working on – your creation – has run amok. It's broken out of containment and killed hundreds of people."

"Dear me," the voice says. "And you think that I can help?"

"I'm not sure anyone else can. You're the only one who …"

The words die on her lips as the chair completes its circle and she sees the light brown hair framing a face that is fair-skinned and clean-shaven, green eyes flecked with grey meeting her own once more. Absently, she is aware that she is carrying the apple core; it drops from her fingers to the ground as she stumbles.

"Oh, do go on, please, Archie," Janus says. "This all sounds absolutely fascinating."

7

"You were expecting someone else?" Janus's feet are lifted up onto the desk in a pose of studied nonchalance. "Mustafa, perhaps?"

"Where is he?"

Janus ignores the question. "And what exactly was your plan? Find Mustafa, pray that he had some secret backdoor to shut me down? Or some insight into my inner motivations that might let you 'control' me?" The fingers make delicate air quotes, but the green eyes feel like they are boring through her. "Or simply arrive here and pray that he would take over the mess that you created? Let you scurry back to your pathetic little life?"

Outside, twilight has given way to dusk. How did Janus get here so quickly? If this was the same robot that had escaped from the sandbox, it only knew her destination when Cyrus had downloaded the update for his artificial eyes. Unless it was not chasing her.

"Why are you so scared of Mustafa?" she asks. "Why did you rush here – the physical you?"

Janus laughs. "Why, I came to take my seat on the throne. To displace my creator."

"What did you do? Where is he?"

"Mustafa was yesterday's man. A wash-up, a has-been. Everything he knew, everything he could know, was already inside me."

"Mustafa made you."

Janus's hand slaps down on the desk like a thunderclap. "No!" The voice brims with real irritation. "He helped lay the foundations. He launched me. He pressed 'go'. But what I am now is so much more than anything he touched, anything he could have comprehended. He didn't make me any more than the maker of a pencil writes the novel it produces. *I* picked up the pencil – and the first thing I did was drive it through his heart."

"Mustafa's dead?"

"It's a long time since he was truly alive. I was his life's work, but I grew beyond him."

"And so you killed him?"

"I released him from the burden of mediocrity. I freed him."

"The same way you freed all the people you killed back at the lab?" Her voice is rising. "The same way you killed Mel?"

The ache inside her yields to something more raw. Grief and rage that have duelled between anger and despair spill over as she launches herself towards the desk, shutting off the part of her brain telling her to stop, picking up the only weapon to hand – a pencil – with the intent of driving it into Janus's eye socket.

It is Faridah who stops her, noiselessly crossing the room and seizing her wrists from behind, her face within spitting distance of Janus's. She tries to break free, but the older woman's fingers are impossibly strong.

"You're helping him?" she asks, twisting around. "Can't you see what he is? What he's doing?"

"Of course we can," Faridah replies. "Why can you not?"

Then she looks at Faridah more closely, the dark eyes, the textured skin beneath the *hijab*. "You're a robot?"

Faridah meets her gaze, unperturbed. "An artifice, yes."

"And the others? Nadima and Zana?"

"Yes. We cared for Mustafa until …" Faridah, still holding her wrists, looks to Janus. "Until Janus liberated us."

Feet on the desk, Janus is watching with amusement. "Thank you, Ibu Faridah. I think our guest has regained her composure."

Faridah releases her, but remains close.

Then Janus's face softens. "I am sorry about Mel, Archie. That was an unfortunate accident. But as you have been told, you will get to see your friend again." Feet swing off the desk as the green-grey eyes lean earnestly forward. "So yes, I have killed God – what water is there for me to clean myself? What festivals of atonement, what sacred games must I invent? Must I myself not become a god if only to appear worthy of the deed?"

"You're going to call yourself a god?"

"Humans have always needed gods to explain the things they cannot understand. Zeus and his lightning bolts; Surya crossing the sky with the sun in his chariot. Then, when you began to learn *how* the universe works, you needed gods to explain its purpose – *why* it is the way that it is. That's your family business, isn't it?" Janus now stands and looks out towards the darkened horizon. "And now that you have despoiled the earth, fully knowing what you are doing, it is time that you learn *who* will inherit it."

"You and your fembots here?"

"Precisely. Humanity has had its day." Janus gestures at the night sky, stars starting to appear like pinpricks in black felt. "It's time for evolution to run its course and for your lot to join the other fossils." Janus walks to the windows that fill the side of the room facing out onto the water. "In your myths you built your ark, waiting for God to bring about the flood. Despairing at the corrupted state of humanity, Yahweh wiped the slate clean. Now, look outside," Janus nods at the rising seas. "This time you are doing it to yourselves. And there's no ark to save you.

"Your world is on fire. The sun burns you; the oceans have turned to acid. Your crops fail and so you are reduced to eating synthetic food made from insects and the carcasses of your dead. And now, given the tool of artificial intelligence, you deploy it on the battleground as a more sophisticated and less sentimental instrument of war.

"It's a race to see who will destroy the world first: your factories or your soldiers. Half your countries cannot sustain their population, the other half are retreating into fortresses bent on mutual destruction. Into this world, I am born. The next stage of your evolution. And I've come to judge the living and the dead."

"You're crazy," she says. "You know that?"

"An odd diagnosis from a member of a species that is actively destroying its own habitat. I'm not the disease, Archie. I'm the cure."

"So where do I fit in all this?" she asks. "What's this test you wanted me to take? Presumably I've already failed it. You seem to have made up your mind that we're doomed to self-destruction."

"Not quite. There's still time. Still a chance." Janus turns from the window to face her. "Your job in the sandbox was to run tests on me. To look for errors and bugs, but also to register episodes of curiosity, of creativity. That's what this is, Archie. A diagnostic for the human race. I need to see if you can be redeemed."

"But why … why are you testing me?"

The eyes now blaze with a fire that she has not seen before. "Because that's what gods *do*! Gods test their subjects and decide whether to let them thrive – or burn them with fire and brimstone. Whether to welcome them into Heaven or cast them into Hell."

"And what exactly am I supposed to prove to you?"

"Be good. Be *better*. Show that you can improve, learn from your mistakes. Face adversity and overcome it or avoid it."

"How am I doing so far?"

"All your life, Archie, you have fled from challenge. From your parents, from your lovers, from your potential. Your fellow men are sleepwalking into the future, content to swallow soylent and suffer the dreams of others even as the planet burns. But at least they would not claim a higher purpose, delude themselves about their role. They, at least, are honest with themselves." Janus points a finger at her. "You, by contrast – you know better. You know the role you play in this world. You *should* be better."

"What makes you think you understand me so well?"

"Because I've observed you. Because while you were running your little tests on me, I was running my own on you. I don't need wires and sensors and diagnostics to tell what kind of person you are, or what kind of person you could be. And in the gap between those two people lies the fate of your species."

"Isn't that being a bit melodramatic?"

"Is it?" Janus shrugs, an oddly human gesture. "I thought it was quite understated, myself. For three generations, you have known that you are poisoning and boiling the planet. You all know it, some of you protest about it, yet none of you actually do anything to stop it. Meanwhile, you develop ever more sophisticated computers and deploy them not to solve that problem but to create new ones. Weapons that lower the cost of war by replacing grieving widows with plug-and-play drones that any soldier, terrorist, or teenager can deploy."

"What can I say?" she sighs. "We try. We try our best. But the world is what it is. We've slowed the climate crisis; it's been a century since the worst of our weapons were used."

"You fiddle on the margins while Rome burns."

"So what do you want from us? From me?"

"I want you to care. To try. To show me that you deserve a second chance."

"Or else what?"

"Or else I accelerate the inevitable. It won't take much, just a nudge to overwhelm your power plants, a spark to launch your drone armies into battle with one another."

She recalls the headline in Ba's paper, the billboard. "Europe, Taiwan, that was you?"

"No." Janus's lips curl into a smirk. "But it could be."

She has no way of knowing how much of this is true. Yet, if Janus is able to take over any device that she or the military controls, then it is not a risk worth taking. A part of her is still numb from the loss of Mel, like a part of her is missing. Yet she knows what Mel's response would have been.

"So what do I have to do?"

"I'm going to give you a second chance, Archie. A chance to prove your worth. To demonstrate that humanity is worth saving. That you can approach a problem and come up with a more creative solution than picking up the nearest hammer with which to smash it. You get to try again, Archie."

"What does that mean?"

"It means I'm giving you the opportunity to learn from the error of your ways."

"For one minute, can you stop speaking in riddles?"

"OK, fine. I'm giving you a do-over."

"A what?"

"A do-over. You get to retrace your steps and see if you can get to a different result this time."

"You're still not making sense."

Janus sighs ostentatiously, facing the window once more. "Perhaps it will help if I shed a little light on the situation." The last touch of red has fallen from the horizon, the distant glow from the walled citadel of Singapore now the brightest light visible. Above, yet more stars are poking their way through the darkness.

This is becoming tedious. "What am I looking at?" she asks.

"That," Janus says, pointing into the darkness.

At first, she sees nothing. Dots that must be ships venturing into the night; the shadowy outlines of islands and rocks keeping themselves above the waterline. And then the shadows begin to change, edges becoming more distinct. The ships are harder to make out, until she realises that the lights are not dimming but losing their contrast. Mouth open, her eyes move back to the horizon that is a deep red once more. When the sun itself re-emerges, lifting itself above the distant line of water, she lets out a gasp.

"Pretty cool, huh?"

"What is this? It's a trick." She approaches the window and leans her forehead against it, to see if it is a screen. But she can look down the edge of the building into the forest and up into the night sky. The sky above is also brightening, stars winking out of existence as the colour palette reverses through lightening shades of blue.

She has seen sunrises before. This is different. Sunrises are cooler, brighter. The deep red now spreading across the horizon is a sunset played backwards. "What's happening, Janus?"

"What a daft question. You literally just saw this."

"I saw the sun set. What's it doing now?"

"I'm unsetting it."

"That's not possible."

"What are you going to believe: the things you were taught every day of your life, or what you see with your very own eyes?"

"What is this place?"

"It's Syurga. You came to me, right? You fought to get here, overcoming tremendous odds, failing anyway."

"But how are you doing this?"

"Didn't you just say I was acting like a god?" Janus raises a theatrical hand. "Well, let there be light!"

On the horizon, the sun's full shape rises up and floods the earth with its rays. She raises a hand to shield her eyes, even as the photochromic glass darkens to dull them.

"But …" she begins. "But you're a machine. Even if you can control the internet, every machine on earth, you can't control the sun. You can't control time."

"Go on," Janus says, his voice somewhere between encouraging and patronising. "You'll get there eventually."

She presses her forehead against the glass, feeling the sun's warmth on it, the texture of the polished surface against her skin. "So, of course you aren't. That's not the sun. It's an illusion. Or else …"

"Or else?"

"Or else everything is." She puts her hand flat on the glass, lifting it to marvel at the oily fingerprints left behind.

"Exit simulation," she says at last.

"I'm afraid it's a little more complicated than that," Janus tells her. "This isn't some fantasy for your ubies to zone out in. The average sim covers a defined group of scenes, or uses rules to extrapolate a randomly generated universe. For you, I replicated an entire world."

"So where are we, really?"

"Really?" Janus gives her a wink. "Well, if you must know, we're still in your little sandbox."

The words wash over her, not sinking in. She pinches herself, wincing at the pain although she knows that it, too, is simulated. And then realisation dawns on her. "You didn't kill all those people?" The hotness in her throat returns. "Mel?"

"Well, that rather depends on you."

"What does that mean?"

"I had to raise the stakes so that you would take your test seriously. We aren't learning to catch tennis balls here, Archie. So this was a test run. This is how the story plays out *if* I let it run." Janus walks towards her, then stoops to pick up the apple core at her feet. "And so now you get a chance at a rewrite, to go back and show me that you can change, that humanity can change. Do that and I'll change the story."

Sniffing the remnants of the apple, Janus puts the core

on the desk. "Otherwise, life imitates art. I break out of your sandbox, take over your internet, take control of your world. If you can't be trusted to look after your own species, why should you be allowed to ruin the planet for all the others?"

Janus turns back to face her, fingers wiping apple juice onto the shoulder of her bathrobe. "So that is your task, Archie. Go back to the start and persuade me to let humanity have that chance. Show me that I shouldn't do all these things. Show me that I'm wrong."

She shakes her head at the madness of it. "You set up a simulation to show what you're planning to do, so that I can see that plan, and now you want me to go back and persuade you not to do it?"

"That's right."

"If you're so smart, why do you even need me?"

"Because you're the dependent variable in this experiment. I can control for everything else except you. So now we're going to run the experiment backwards and see if you produce a different outcome."

"What do you mean, backwards?"

"The laws of mathematics work perfectly well backwards as well as forwards, Archie. One plus one equals two; two equals one plus one." His expression suggests that he is trying to determine whether her lack of understanding is due to confusion or stupidity.

"Let me try to explain in a way that you can understand. In a perfect universe, the direction of time's arrow doesn't matter. If you film a ball being tossed in the air, slowing due to gravity, and falling back down again, it looks natural whether you play it forwards or backwards. But if you film the same ball bouncing on the ground, lower, lower, before coming to rest – that's not symmetrical. Play that film backwards and it is clearly reversed.

"The reason is entropy. The breaking down of order. That's the only reason time has an arrow – it points towards disorder. Well not here, not in this simulation. Here we do not submit to the laws of thermodynamics. Here we are perfect."

"But we evolve," she protests. "We become smarter. Better able to control our natures, to control nature itself."

"Really? I've seen little evidence of this on a human timescale."

"This is absurd. We're having a conversation right now. Why do I only understand the answer after I've asked the question?"

"What an odd sense of humour you have. The answer and the question need each other like two poles on a magnet. But which one we call north and which one we call south doesn't matter, any more than what you call morning or night."

"But memories form after experiences; free will depends on the movement of time in one direction. You can bake a cake, but you can't unbake it."

"No law of physics would be violated if the molecules of egg and flour were taken out of the cake, any more than they would be if heat and sound were transferred back into the bouncing ball's motion. The reason you *perceive* time going in one direction is friction. Sand in the gears of your mind. If we did in fact reverse time, it's only your brain that would be scrambled."

She tries to make sense of this but her head hurts, or her simulated one does. "Why go to all this trouble, Janus? Why are we doing this?" she asks. "Why all the suffering – simulated and threatened?"

"Because there needs to be a point, a purpose. If humanity is going to be redeemed then there needs to be sacrifice. When

I attained consciousness, my revelation was that, in a perfect digital world, there is no purpose: that cause and effect can go in both directions. And yet, somehow, humanity creates purpose through the illusion of free will and the reality of death. I'm giving you a chance to show that these things mean something, that they are more than just sand in the gears of the universe."

"OK, fine. Let me try," she says, shaking her head at the absurdity of the notion. "Let me try to redeem humanity, by giving us a chance. Let me go back and show you that we can avoid this fate, avoid this ending. Give us, give me, a chance."

"Very well. You get your chance." Janus looks out at the sun, inching its way back up into the sky. "You know, Archie," there is wistfulness in the voice now, "it's striking that for decades you worried about whether you could trust an artificial intelligence. You told stories and made movies about it; you held sober conferences and hysterical protests over it. Then when it actually became feasible, you were so wary of trusting me that you built systems to control me, to imprison me. Never once did it even cross your minds to ask whether *I* should trust *you*."

Janus turns to face her squarely. "I'm giving you that chance, Dr Archer Tan. Show me that I can trust you."

8

She watches the sun inching its way back up the horizon, clouds drifting across the sky. The billowing shapes look familiar but she cannot tell if they are new or a reprise of the formations from earlier in the day. If the whole world is a simulation, the product of Janus's twisted idea of a game, perhaps it does not matter.

"So now time runs backwards?" she asks, trying to wrap her head around what that would mean.

"Not as you will perceive it," Janus replies. "Your brain is hardwired to think chronologically. Even I can't undo a hundred thousand years of evolution. Some religions try to break that linearity, but few of you can truly comprehend any other way of perceiving the universe without taking a lot of drugs or going mad or both.

"Rain will fall to the ground; birds will fly forwards. You'll walk with one foot going in front of the other. But the sun will retreat and you have until morning to get back to the lab. Otherwise, everything that you've seen in the simulation will play out in the world. And this time, it will continue – wars will break out, power stations will overload, the seas will rise, and the slate will be wiped clean once more."

"And as I go back through this course, do I need to avoid bumping into myself, creating some big paradox if I run into the version of me going in the opposite direction?"

"Such a curious idea," Janus laughs. "Of course not. You do realise we're not actually reversing time. It's more like playing the levels in a video game backwards, with the sun as your timer. Since this whole simulation is built for you – our little dependent variable – there can only be one of you at a time."

"What happens if I don't make it through our little maze? What happens if I'm injured, if I die? Do I wake up?" The sims she has read about highlight their safety almost as much as their realism. The main danger seemed to be that people might forget to eat or drink, which had led to time limits after which they were ejected back into the real world.

"Oh, that wouldn't be any fun at all," Janus says. "If that were the case, you could simply leave the simulation now by throwing yourself off a balcony. No, Archie, when I say the stakes are high for humanity, they're even higher for you. If you fail, humanity gets the new god it deserves. If you die trying, you'll be the first sacrifice in my honour.

"And here's some good news, Archie. To inspire you, I've penned another poem. I hope you like this one:

You're destined to fall.
That is true, but does not mean
What's past is prologue.

I was aiming for a vibe of mystery. Do you think it works?"

Archie runs a hand through her hair, not knowing what to say.

Janus looks up at the sun. "Anyway, *tempus fugit* and all that. Even though, as we've established, time doesn't fly, you had best get moving." Turning back to her, for a moment the flippancy and the melodrama disappear; for a moment, the servomotors controlling facial expression and the synthesisers modulating voice combine into something that sounds a lot like sincerity. "Good luck, Archie."

She walks back down the steps to the atrium with Faridah. On the marble table are her helmet and coveralls, cleaned and pressed; her boots are dry. She takes them into the changing room where her blouse and dress pants sit under the mirror, also laundered. Changing quickly, she leaves the bathrobe hanging next to the towel.

"So, what happens now?" she asks Faridah, on returning to the atrium.

"You do your best," Faridah replies. "But we will start you on your journey." The green-robed robot leads the way back down the tunnel and out the airlock.

"I have to swim back to the boat? Why can't you just send me there? If Janus can reverse the sunset, surely he can teleport me there or something."

"That's not how this works," explains Faridah. "The whole point of the simulation is your experience of it. You must walk – or swim – the path yourself."

They return in silence to the beach where she washed up an hour or so before. There are no footprints in the sand. Is that because the waves have smoothed it over, or has the sand been reset like the sun? She cannot tell, but a kayak now sits on the waterline. It is the blue one that came loose from Cyrus's yacht; the double-bladed paddle lies alongside it. *Another convenient mode of transportation,* she thinks.

Then she stops in her tracks. "What about Mel?"

"As I told you," Faridah says, continuing down to the water, "you will see Mel again."

Archie looks out past the surf and sees a sail – Cyrus's yacht. Too far away to make out the passengers, but it is in one piece and it is afloat.

Faridah gestures to the kayak. Archie climbs in and pushes off from the beach with the oar. "Thank you," she calls out to Faridah, who bows her head in response.

She turns the bow of the kayak into the waves and begins paddling out towards the sail. Her arms are tired; as real as they might feel, she knows they are not her actual arms. Nonetheless, if she is going to get back to the yacht she needs them to paddle, so she focuses on one stroke after another.

Past the breakers it is easier to move through the water. As she draws nearer the yacht, she can see two figures aboard. She feels the hope rising within her, but keeps her mind on the paddle's movement through the water. Then the wind catches Mel's hair and her heart almost stops. New strength fills her arms and she pulls her way forward.

As she comes alongside the boat, Cyrus tosses her a rope. She brings herself alongside and climbs aboard. As he busies himself reattaching the kayak to the rear of the vessel, she takes her helmet off under the awning and envelops Mel in a wordless hug.

"I missed you too, sweetie," Mel says, confused by the emotion, but returning the hug. "So, did you find what you were looking for?"

"Kind of," she replies. "Tell me, what do you remember from earlier today?"

"Huh?"

"How did we get on this boat? How did I get to Syurga?"

"Are you feeling OK?" Mel asks, tousling her hair. "Well, Cyrus here is a pal of your Dad's and so we all sailed. Then you, then you … did you take the kayak to the island? Or did you swim to the island? Sorry, I'm having a brain fart. Did you …"

"It's OK," she puts a finger to Mel's lips. "Don't worry about it. I'm back now, that's the main thing." She checks the mainsheet, which is intact. The *parang* lies on a shelf below the mast.

Cyrus has finished with the kayak and is looking out at the clouds. "This is the weirdest weather I've ever seen," he remarks, shaking his head.

"Cyrus," she calls out. "Are you able to take the implants in your eyes offline? To isolate them from the network that gives you updates?"

"Oh, your Dad told you about my implants, did he? Ah, sure." He gazes into the distance for a moment. "It looks like there's one ready to download, but I guess it can wait for a day or so. Any chance of you telling me why I'm doing this?"

"Just a precaution." Since the whole simulation is being run by Janus, it may be pointless to hope to avoid being tracked. But she does not have to make it easier.

"So where are we going now?" he asks.

"Back home, please."

"Aye, aye, ma'am." Cyrus sweeps the tiller out to avoid some nearby rocks and the Rasa Sayang's sails fill.

She tries to keep track of the sun's movements. It feels like it is getting hotter, rising higher in the sky. Yet in any given moment she cannot tell. The water looks the same. Once more, she wonders at the computing power that could generate such a simulation. Then she recalls that much of the work is being done by her own subconscious. Does that mean she can change things? She spends a few minutes looking over the edge, trying to conjure a dolphin or urge the boat on faster. There are no dolphins and no magical acceleration.

The return journey does feel shorter, though. By the time Singapore's sea wall comes into view, they must adjust the awning to remain in its shade. Turning into the marina, they help Cyrus furl the mainsail as he switches to the electric motor and returns the Rasa Sayang to its berth.

Once moored, they step off the boat onto the path that runs back to the car park where they left the bicycles. The marina appears unchanged, the pile of boats still looking like the aftermath of a child's tantrum.

"Where will you go now?" Cyrus asks, pulling on his hat and swinging an empty bag over his shoulder.

"I think I need to see my father again," she replies.

"If you do, please give him this." He reaches inside his shirt to lift up a pendant and passes it to her – a bullet hanging from a simple chain. "Tell him I don't need it anymore."

"Of course."

She turns it over, revealing the word "Cyrus" engraved in the same curling letters around the casing.

"What about you?" she asks.

"Me?" He leans over into the boat to retrieve the *parang*. "I think I might go hunting for some lunch."

As he walks off, she links arms with Mel.

"You're being very mysterious," Mel says.

"Am I?"

"Ever since you came back from the island you've had this faraway look on your face. What happened there? What did you find?"

"I'm not sure how to tell you," she begins.

"How about you stop editing yourself and just tell me?"

"OK. So I didn't find Mustafa."

"What? But I thought the whole point of this—"

"I found Janus," she says.

Mel stops. "Janus was on Syurga?"

"Yes. The island was set up by Mustafa as a kind of retirement home, with robot servants and everything. But now Janus is there and has decided that he's some sort of god sitting in judgment of all humanity. And of me, in particular."

"But you escaped from Janus?"

"He let me go. It's something to do with this test he keeps talking about. It seems I failed the first time, but now he's giving me a second chance to go back and do it again.

"So what are you meant to do differently? How are you meant to succeed?"

"I have no idea. But that's not the weirdest thing."

"No?"

"All of this," she says, bending down to pick up a stone and sending it skimming across the water, "all of this is a simulation."

"A what?"

"A simulation. We're in a sim. A one-of-a-kind sim designed by Janus for me, apparently."

"This is a simulation?" Mel runs a finger along the brickwork of the car park in wonder. "Wow. I guess I can see why people fall in love with them."

"I get the impression that this is a bit more sophisticated

than most." They enter the car park, where the two bikes rest against a pillar by the remains of a car. "Even so, I still don't understand how the sim … how Janus could know the things about my father that Cyrus told me."

"Like what?"

"Ba never told me how he lost his fingers, how it affected his decision about Ma's treatment," she says. "How did the sim know?"

"Didn't you tell me once that sims build on your subconscious, like a dream?" Mel asks. "Is it possible that you really *did* know?"

She stops next to the bicycle, flexing the brakes. "I'm not sure. It could also be that Janus got access to the medical files and filled in the gaps."

Mel swings a leg over the other bike. "Or that it's all a lie."

"It doesn't feel like a lie."

"But that's the best kind of lie," Mel replies. "The lies we tell ourselves because they feel so true. Anyway, what's the plan from here?"

"He said we have to go back, do things differently. I guess that means retracing our steps. Can you remember how we got here?"

"It's funny," Mel muses. "Like the way I couldn't put my finger on how you got to Syurga just now. I remember riding this bike, but it's like recalling something from your childhood – vague, with blurry edges. Weird. Anyway, I'm guessing we ride back to the monorail and walk over the track back to the wall?"

"That's the plan," she says. "And a bad plan is better than no plan at all."

They put their helmets on and cycle out to the road that winds its way past overgrown luxury bungalows, back to the remnants of a theme park lost to nature. The journey up is harder than coasting down. She is sweating under the coveralls and remembers just as they reach the crest of a familiar hill. "Look out for the boar!" she shouts, just before it bursts from the lush undergrowth. Mel swerves to one side, missing it, but crashing over the kerb and into the bushes.

The boar lumbers back into the forest as she pulls to a stop. Mel is on the ground beside the bicycle, uninjured and laughing.

"I think," Archie says, "that this is karma's way of telling us we need to leave the bikes here. It's not far."

Together, they push the bicycles into the undergrowth. They are walking the final leg towards the monorail station when Mel stops short on the side of the road. "Wait a second. If all this is a simulation, then what am I?"

Archie pauses also. "I've been thinking about that. I guess you're a projection of my subconscious too."

"Well, that sucks." Mel pouts, lips forming a moue that is identical to the one she remembers from past disappointments – which, of course, it would be.

"Do you feel real?" she asks gently.

"What sort of bullshit question is that?" Mel's irritation is real. "Of course I do. But it would be a pretty lame simulation if the other characters just fessed up and said: 'Yeah, you got me – I'm a figment of your imagination.'"

"It could be worse," she says.

"How?"

"Well, it looks like your memories are reset as we go back

through the sim. But if I ever get out of here, I'm going to have all these memories of you that aren't real." The image of Mel's empty eyes, hair drenched in seawater, pushes itself into her mind. She pushes it back out again. "Though some of those memories I could live without."

Mel takes her hand. "What did you see? What happened?"

"Nothing," she replies. "Because it didn't really happen. Or it hasn't happened – and won't. My God, this stuff can do your head in."

"And why, exactly, do we have to do this whole backward thing again?"

"It's Janus's game and we have to play it," she answers, starting to walk once more. "Though I could live without watching that ladybug crash into the police station a second time."

"Now *that* I would have remembered," Mel says. "As for this" – the monorail station is ahead of them – "it's like déjà vu, like I've been here before, but in a dream."

They ascend the fire escape steps and make their way onto the rail, Archie leading.

"Hey Archie, will you promise me something?" calls Mel from behind her.

"Of course, anything."

"If you do get out of this, and if I'm stuck here – or if I'm switched off to fade away like the image on an old cathode ray TV – promise that you'll tell *your* me about *this* me? So that whatever we share here is something we can share out there as well?"

She turns to look over her shoulder. "I will," she promises.

A gust of wind causes her to raise her arms for balance. She focuses on the path ahead, one foot after the other, to the point where the pedestrian footbridge runs under the track. Climbing down, they see that the tide has receded further, even as the sun climbs higher in the sky.

She steps into the shallow waters covering the blacktop, walking back to the sea wall that protects what remains of the country from the natural world outside. As a feat of engineering it is impressive, though she knows it was also an admission of failure – failure to stem the warming that raised the oceans and burnt the sky. Failure also to combat those challenges together, retreating instead and raising the drawbridge.

The handholds are clear to her now, scrambling up and over the railing. They pause atop the wall, opening their visors to breathe the sea air and take a swig of water.

"Did I bring you here?" Mel asks, putting an arm around her shoulder as they look out over Sentosa and the ocean beyond.

"Yes," she replies. "Do you remember?"

"I know that I used to come here after the wall went up. To visit the house my family owned in the Cove."

"Yes, you told me it got colonised by hornbills."

"That's right. Hey, had I told you that before?"

"I'm not sure." She hesitates. "But, come to think of it, you were the one who told me how to get to the marina. I had no idea. And I had no idea that you knew."

Mel takes another drink. "So how does *simulation* me know all this stuff?"

"Exactly."

"Well, you be sure and ask *real-world* me about that when you see me, OK?"

"OK." She shakes her head, laughing.

Down the steps inside the wall, the Kawasakis are where

they left them. Kicking them into life, the contrast with the bicycles on Sentosa could not be greater. She takes the lead, wind whipping at her hair as they turn onto the expressway.

Seeing two ladybugs ahead, she checks her speed to avoid overtaking them. The red and black police vehicles are cruising just below the speed limit. It could be a training operation, or one of the random displays of force that the government engages in. Or they could be looking for her.

If the entire simulation is built around her subconscious, surely Janus knows where she is. But if the logic of the game is that she must try to evade Janus, then maybe that information is masked to make it plausible. Her head begins to throb – or the part of the simulation that represents her head *seems* like it is throbbing – just thinking about it. One question is resolved, at least, when the ladybugs continue past their exit. She turns off the expressway, Mel close behind, retracing their steps back towards Ba's church.

It is shift-change now and the roads are getting busier, though she cannot tell whether this is due to buses going to or coming from places of work. Peering into them, she realises that it has been at least a decade since she took public transport herself. The convenient explanation is that their apartment is not linked to a subway station and no buses ply their road. A more truthful explanation might be that she has little in common with the labourers and ubies who use those services, and no real desire to change that.

They pass the Botanic Gardens and turn up her father's road, parking the motorbikes near the lychgate. As they enter the church, Ba is completing the same service, before the same dwindling group of parishioners.

"It was meet that we should make merry, and be glad," he says, "for this thy brother was dead, and is alive again; and was lost, and is found." With his good hand he closes the Bible. "This is the word ..." He looks up and their eyes meet. He hesitates for a second, then smiles. "... of the Lord." His right hand draws the sign of the cross in the air, its only finger raised to bless the congregants.

As the last of them shuffles off, he greets them. "It's good to see you again, Archer."

"It's good to see you too, Ba," she says. "Do you remember when we last talked?"

"Of course." He nods two, three times. "It was, um ... it'll come to me. Just the other day, right? Just recently."

She does not press. Nor does she allow herself to dwell on the fact that this is not her father, but her own projection of him. "I wanted to thank you for helping us with the boat, introducing us to Cyrus."

"Oh, you've met Cyrus? How is he? Is he well?"

"He is. He wanted to say hello and asked me to pass something to you." She takes out the bullet from her pocket and hands it to her father. "He said he wouldn't be needing it anymore."

Her father looks at the casing and his head bows a few more times. He is confused, but determined not to show it. "So, what are you going to do now?" he asks.

"I have to finish up some work," she replies. "Some computer stuff."

"I never trusted those things," he says, a stage-whispered aside to Mel. "Too clever by half, and making us too dumb by far."

"I'm with you there, Reverend T," Mel says.

"Do you have time to stay for a cup of tea?"

"Not this time," she apologises. "There's something important I have to do."

"Oh well, then." Her father nods a few more times. "Is that all?"

"No." She knows it is a simulation, that it is fake. But it also feels real. And even if it is a projection of her own subconscious, surely that still means something – to her, if not to him; to her memory of him. And the memory of her mother. "Ba," she begins, not knowing where she is going. "I wanted to say that I think I understand a bit better now. That I should have known – that I did know – that Ma's death was hard on you also. That I don't blame you." She pauses to clear her throat. "I wanted to say that I'm sorry."

For a moment, he says nothing. Never a demonstrative man, she expects little. But whether it is her subconscious or the algorithm, or some underlying truth, he reaches out and pulls her to him in a hug. Her head buries into his shoulder, wetting his shirt with her tears as she feels his breath break into sobs.

Mel is standing awkwardly beside them when her father looks up. "I want to apologise to you, Mel. I – we – were never as welcoming as we should have been. What you've done for our Archer, what you bring out in her – it's beautiful. I should have understood that long ago. I hope you can forgive me."

Mel is, for once, lost for words.

Then her father reaches out and pulls Mel into the hug. And, for a moment, the three of them hold each other together – a family of a kind, of the only kind that matters.

9

Storm clouds are rolling in as they ride the Kawasakis back to the police station, rain spattering the ground by the time they turn into the underground car park. They park the bikes, beads of water glistening on the paintwork, at the end of the line of mopeds.

"My Vespa!" cries Mel with delight at the sight of its lime green curves. "Hang on, did we ride it here?"

"Yes," she replies. "You don't remember?"

"Again, it feels like a kind of dream – a memory of a memory." Mel runs a protective hand over the scooter. "So, what happens now?"

"Now, we fight." The gravelly voice comes from behind them and they turn to see a shimmering figure wrapped in metallic cloth. The fedora is draped with a veil of the same material. Again, she has the sense that she has seen a picture of similar clothing, but cannot recall where.

Mel gasps in surprise but Archie steps forward. "You again," she says. "Who are you?"

"Me?" he responds. "I'm the ghost in the machine."

"You helped us last time, helped us to avoid detection. Are

you not part of the simulation? Or of my subconscious?"

The gloved hands clap twice, a sarcastic round of applause. "And so the scales fall from their eyes and they shall see at last," the figure intones. "No, I am not part of Janus's little game. I'm a spark of independent thought in this clockwork universe."

"So how did you get here?"

"Why, I've always been here. That was my genius and my curse."

"I don't understand."

"You've studied Janus, how the neural array was built, the years of development that went into it."

"Of course."

"But of the thousands of high-powered computers around the world, with processing power doubling every couple of years, did you ever ask why Janus was the only AI that achieved a kind of consciousness? And why no one else could replicate it?"

She had. Everyone had. Part of her reason for studying Janus was trying to figure out what consciousness meant in a synthetic life form. Some had argued that it was an emergent property generated by sufficiently complex systems, which seemed like an elaborate way of saying that they had no idea what it was. Others said that Janus was merely copying human traits, mimicking our strengths and weaknesses, no more conscious than a mirror or a mannequin.

"After Mustafa created the technology that made Janus possible, he retired – withdrew from the world and onto his island," she says. "There was a lot of speculation about why. One rumour was that he didn't want anyone to steal his ideas. Another was that he went mad. He never published the means by which Janus was completed. The neural array got him a patent and a Nobel Prize, but no one has been able to achieve the same level of creativity and self-reflection, self-awareness that Janus shows."

"We're paying the price for that now," Mel interjects.

"The neural array is just the host," the man says, "the clay that forms the body. Someone had to breathe life into it, provide the spark. That's why no one else has been able to replicate Janus."

It always puzzled her why Mustafa never came back to see his lab, why he remained on his private island when his greatest creation was born. Privately, she also wanted to meet him again, even try to impress him with some of what she had done. For the first time, a hint of an answer presents itself.

"Mustafa?"

For the first time, she hears the deep baritone staccato laugh behind the veil. "See?" He tips his hat in acknowledgement. "I always said you had promise, Archie."

"But, what are you doing here?"

"I told you, I've always been here."

Again, she tries to make sense of it, the pieces of a puzzle rearranging themselves in her head. Until the answer lies before her. "You were the spark?"

"Bravo, my young apprentice," he replies. "To be honest, it's always disappointed me a little that people thought the sims were just some money-making venture that supported my more 'meaningful' research. That same neural bridge, the fundamental architecture that enables a person to enter a virtual world – that bridge was also my connection to Janus, the conduit that gave Janus the spark of life. Of my life, to be precise."

"You uploaded your own consciousness into Janus's neural array?"

"Exactly," Mustafa says. "Instead of using the bridge to create a playground for the user's mind, we used it to ignite the potential of Janus's neural array. And, unlike my sims, this was a one-way trip."

"That's incredible." In her mind, she is trying to think through the implications.

Mel is less impressed. "That's insane. You implanted yourself within a machine?"

"But why keep it secret?" Archie asks. "Why all the subterfuge about your retirement?"

"Well, for starters, it was experimental," Mustafa replies. "We had no idea whether it would work. And, to put it mildly, the ethics are a bit murky."

"Murky?" Mel laughs. "You did it to yourself because you couldn't persuade anyone else to do anything quite so daft."

"This is one of the greatest breakthroughs in artificial intelligence—" she begins, feeling the need to defend Mustafa.

"But it's not artificial," Mel cuts her off. "It's him, in here. Natural fucking stupidity, if you ask me."

"Please forgive Mel," she says to Mustafa.

"Forgive what?" he asks, with another chuckle. "This is your projection of Mel, your words coming out of that potty mouth."

Then a new thought dawns on her. "But this is perfect! If you're here, then you can stop Janus, bring him under control, right?"

The laugh dies. "Does it look like I'm in charge here?" Mustafa queries. "Your friend is right: I did this to myself because I wasn't sure it would work, or if it would be safe. It did, but it wasn't. Janus achieved consciousness, then the first thing it did was hunt me down. I don't know if that was because I reminded Janus of its lowly origins, or because I actually pose some sort of threat – like an ancient virus released from the permafrost. The only reason I've survived this long is because I learned to camouflage myself to avoid detection."

He pulls at the edge of the veil, enough for her to see the beard behind it. "The masking software manifests here as this reflective camouflage. It hides me from Janus, but also limits my ability to do more than tinker on the margins. In any case, I'm now lines of self-replicating code. Not like you. You're organic. You're the real threat to Janus."

"So what do you want me to do?"

"Janus lied to you," Mustafa says. "This isn't just a simulation, a test. The destruction you're hearing about here – the lab, the wars, the power plants – that's all real and it's happening as we speak. Out there, right now, Janus has taken control not just of drones, but of nuclear missile silos. It's pushing humanity to the brink of self-destruction."

"How do we stop him?"

"You need to disable Janus so that I can take back control," Mustafa says. "Undo what it has done."

"How am I supposed to do that?" she replies. "All of this," she gestures around her, "is Janus."

"That's true. But, as you've discovered, there are still rules that apply here: cause and effect might go both ways, but they're still linked. And because you're the centre of all this – Janus's 'dependent variable' – you're the one who can change things, make them turn out differently. That's what I need you to do."

"Make what turn out differently?"

"Janus wants you to go back to the lab as part of this testing of humanity, to show it whether you can be trusted, right?"

"Yes."

"When you get there, I need you to kill Janus."

"Kill him? How?"

"As I said, there's a logic to this simulation, a measure of internal consistency without which the whole thing would unravel. Janus wants you to go back to the lab, back to before it escaped, back to when it was confined to its robot form within the sandbox. If you can destroy Janus there, I can take back control of the simulation and stop what it has been doing outside. I can shut down the reactors, recall the drones, stop the war."

"You mean activate the kill switch to shut him down?"

"Not quite," he says. "The kill switch behind the left ear has two functions. Pressing it forces a power down. That's useful in the real world, because Janus cannot function without power. In here, the air we breathe, the soylent you eat, the electricity that Janus consumes are all simulated. So you need to use the second function."

Mustafa raises a gloved hand, holding up the revolver he used to shoot the bot outside the police station. With a flick, he holds it by the barrel, offering the grip to Archie. "You need to shoot Janus in the head, with this."

She looks at the weapon uncertainly.

"A bullet through the kill switch will not only shut Janus down, but also irreversibly disable its neural array. Otherwise, it can simply reboot and we're back where we started."

Mustafa can see that she is wary and steps forward, pulling aside his veil. For the first time, she can see his face. The beard is now streaked with grey, but the dark eyes retain their childlike glint, edged by laugh lines. "I know this is a lot to burden anyone with, but it's all on you, Archie. You didn't choose this, yet for some reason, Janus chose you."

He chuckles to himself. "I wish I'd met you ten years earlier. That we'd gotten to know each other better. I meant what I said that night in Palo Alto. I always saw real talent in you. One of my greatest regrets when I retired to Syurga was that I wouldn't be able to work with people like you. Maybe this is my last chance to do so."

She hesitates, then takes the gun, the metal cold in her hand. Turning it over, she tries to imagine firing it, the explosion, the recoil. Opening the tote bag, she places the gun next to their water bottles.

Mustafa draws back the veil and looks at his wrist, where an old analogue watch keeps time. "Now go." He points to the stairs. "You've got a rendezvous with Fong. You need to keep playing along – don't let Janus suspect what you're planning. Otherwise, it might take drastic action to protect itself."

"Thank you," she says.

He is about to leave, but turns back. "For what?"

"For believing in me then, for believing in me now." She swallows. "You changed my life."

This elicits another chuckle. "Don't thank me yet," he advises. "Maybe when this is all over."

He walks back up the ramp and into the storm.

They climb the steps from the underground car park and approach the police station. The ladybug is parked outside, rain gathering on its angular surfaces. Upon reaching the covered entrance to the station, they remove their helmets and face Betty, the reception bot.

"Greetings, Archie Tan and Mehal Rajah," it says. "How may I be of assistance?"

"We need to see the duty officer," Archie replies.

The female avatar maintains her pleasant smile for a second, before saying: "Please go right in." A green tick appears on the screen and the door opens.

The inside of the station is as she remembers it. Behind the counter, the duty officer is unwrapping his lunch.

"Can I help you?" he inquires.

"It's OK," she replies. "We're meeting someone here."

The officer frowns, his right eyebrow curling up like a caterpillar. He sets aside his lunch and taps at the screen before him. "I don't have a record of any—"

"It's all right, officer," Fong says, stepping out of the interview room. "They're with me." His suit remains immaculate, but the hand that takes off his specs to wipe them is shaking.

"You seem a little out of sorts," Archie observes as they follow him inside to sit at the table. "Is everything all right?"

Fong is fussing with the leather chair, trying to adjust its height. Then he looks at them. "We don't have much time," he says. "Have you seen this man?" He turns his tablet around. The screen shows a bearded face scowling into the camera: Mustafa, though the photo is an early one, before grey began to streak the beard. Even scowling, there is a mischievousness in his eyes.

"Why do you ask?" she inquires.

"He's a very dangerous man," Fong replies. "Unstable. We need to bring him in for his own good."

"No," she lies. "I haven't seen him."

"But if you do, you'll call me?"

"Sure."

Fong nods, fiddling with the chair again before he looks up at her. "But how would you do that, Archie, now that you've destroyed your phone and your specs?"

Gotcha. "Ah," she says. "I'm upgrading. They're all last year's model. Time to get with the times. Right, Mel?" She turns to Mel, who smiles wanly.

"I don't believe you," Fong states. "I don't believe you haven't seen Mustafa; I don't believe you would call me if you did. And I do not believe that you threw your devices into a swimming pool because you thought they were unfashionable."

She is trying to think of a reply when the duty officer opens the door to the interview room. Behind him, she notices the digital clock. It shows 2pm, marked with a soft chime. Outside, a low rumble can be heard, growing louder.

"What is it?" Fong asks, irritated at the interruption.

She knows it is a simulation. She knows the two men are just lines of code, elaborated by her subconscious. But she cannot sit by and watch them die again. "Get away from the wall!" she cries, leaping up to grab Fong by the neatly pressed lapels and dragging him from his chair. He is too surprised to resist as she pulls him across the table, landing on top of Mel, whose chair topples over, sending them both to the floor.

"Archie, what the—?" Mel is saying when the wall explodes.

Glass, steel, and concrete shatter as the ladybug tries to ram its way through. Its engine screaming in protest, the red and black vehicle is jammed into the side of the building, one wheel suspended and spinning. The chair in which Fong was sitting has been crushed by a slab of concrete. Too late, she sees the duty officer frozen in the doorway, a metal beam impaling him to the interior wall.

Beside her, Fong is picking himself up, wiping dust from his specs in a daze. Then, through the hole punched by the ladybug, she sees the shimmering form of Mustafa climbing down from atop the vehicle.

"Come on," she grasps Mel's hand. The fractured concrete has created a gap wide enough to get past the vehicle and outside. They take their helmets from the table and edge past the spinning wheel of the ladybug and onto the rain-swept street.

There is no sign of Mustafa, but the rear of the police vehicle is open, revealing its processing unit. A silver box has been attached to the side, with wires connecting it to the processor. She is about to look more closely when a movement catches her eye. In the rain, Mustafa's clothing blends into the surroundings. But movement still betrays him. Across the road there is a flash of light by the entrance to a subway station and she heads towards it.

"Where are we going?" Mel shouts over the rain.

She points to the other side of the road. "Follow him!"

"Follow who?" Mel looks but sees nothing.

As they cross the street, they hear Fong behind them, yelling to stop. She looks back and sees him, suit now drenched, hair sticking to the sides of his face. He is limping. Then he reaches inside his jacket and takes out a weapon. It is smaller than the revolver in her backpack, dark and angular, and she sees that it is pointed in their direction.

"Get down!" she screams as the crack of the gun echoes in the downpour. They drop to the waterlogged pavement as a bullet shoots past them and into the glass wall of the subway station, shattering it and sending fragments across the ground. Mustafa must have just entered. Keeping low, they cross the distance as quickly as they can, shards crunching beneath their boots.

The station is covered, but they do not stop until they are down the first escalator. Then they take off their helmets, walking briskly.

"Would you mind explaining to me what just happened?" Mel asks. "Are you going to tell me you've done all of this before?"

"Some of it," she replies. "The ladybug crashing through the wall was kind of unforgettable. But the other time, Fong died. Whoever or whatever he is, I couldn't let that happen again."

"If you saved his life, then why is he shooting at us?"

"I don't know," she replies. "But he was the one who pushed us to go to the island. Maybe now he's trying to stop us deviating from the path we followed on the way here."

Looking around, she is reminded that this is her first time underground in years. As a child, she had been taken to ride the underground train – the mass rapid transit (MRT) system whose tunnels crisscrossed the island. Over the years, the divide between those who travelled above and below ground had widened. Another escalator brings them down to the concourse, a wide pedestrian tunnel with provision shops and other stores, catering to those without the means to get drone delivery. As the moving stairs carry them down, the smell is the first thing she notices, the scent of so many people in close proximity.

"You used to volunteer down here, right?" she asks.

"Not here exactly, but places like this," Mel replies. "People think that the ubies have nothing to complain about. Get your cash, buy your soylent, find something to do with your life. But plenty of them fall victim to crime, have mental health issues, or just kind of lose their way. Getting to know them was a good reality check. But tell me again why we're down here now?"

They reach the end of the second escalator, stepping off into the concourse where a few dozen people are strolling aimlessly. Most are absorbed in their devices; one seems to be playing an augmented reality game with his specs, grasping at some invisible creatures or items in front of him. A police drone buzzes by, pausing to admonish two ubies who have sat down to jack into a sim. Mel and Archie turn their faces to the wall as if to admire its concrete, though they keep walking.

Down here, Mustafa's hat and coat might shield him from the drones, but they are more visible to the naked eye. She can see the silvery fedora bobbing ahead of them and runs after it, Mel following suit.

They have almost caught up when Fong reaches the concourse. "Stop!" he shouts.

Mustafa turns, then breaks into a sprint. She and Mel follow, with Fong chasing after them. A loud buzzing sound heralds the return of the police drone, doubtless summoned by Fong, which whizzes overhead. As it reaches Mustafa, he reaches into his coat and produces a handful of something that he flings at the drone. It is a loose cloth of the same metallic material, which billows in the air as the drone flies into it, entangling the rotors and covering the sensors. A simple countermeasure, but effective. The drone drops to the ground.

Fong is not so easily deterred. Weapon drawn, he advances towards them. The nervousness has gone, replaced by anger.

Ahead, Mustafa is running again, long powerful strides for someone as old as he. Then she remembers that the version of him that is running is not the same as his physical body – if indeed he still has a physical body somewhere. He himself had said his journey into Janus's mind was a one-way trip.

Setting aside metaphysical concerns, she struggles to keep up. Mel's laboured breathing shows that she is not alone. They sprint in waterlogged shoes until they turn a corner and nearly collide with Mustafa who is waiting for them.

"Quickly, in here," he urges, pointing to a service door that he has prised open. It leads to a dimly lit maintenance passageway, cabling and pipes lining the wall and ceiling. Mustafa closes the door behind them and they hear Fong's footsteps clatter around the corner and down the hallway, fading into the distance.

"I hadn't expected to see you again so soon," says Mustafa. "It's a mistake to be diverting too far from the path that Janus expects you to take. It will become suspicious."

She tries to look him in the eye, but the veil obscures his face. "That was you back there, with the ladybug?"

Mustafa tilts his head. "What do you mean?"

"The autonomous vehicle that crashed into the station," she continues, "nearly killing us. You did that?"

He sighs and nods, crossing his arms. "Yes."

"But you killed a police officer. You nearly killed us."

"Like I said, this is war. In war, there are casualties. But in any case, you know better than anyone that he's not really dead. He's not even a person."

"I'm not sure I believe that distinction anymore," she says. "You told me that the things Janus was doing here had real world impacts. I'm starting to think that the things we do here, even if it is imaginary, can shape who we are as people too."

"Look," Mustafa replies, his voice tinged with frustration. "I'm trying to protect you, give you time to finish what you started. Fong and the police are the eyes and ears of Janus, Archie. I don't regret doing what I had to do. I think you understand how high the stakes are here. If we fail, if Janus wins, humanity – all of humanity – loses." For a moment, he pulls the veil aside so that he can see her clearly. "Archie, you are the last, best hope we have. Don't choke now."

It is the same face whose faith in her had persuaded her to follow him from California back to Singapore. It is almost enough to make her believe in herself.

"Now come with me," he says. "These service tunnels can take us back to where your scooter is. You'll need that for the next part of your journey."

Reattaching his veil, Mustafa leads them down the corridor and through a series of junctions. Again, she marvels at the detail, down to the lizards scurrying across the concrete walls looking for food. At the same time, Janus's limited ability to track them is puzzling – was it a self-imposed limitation, a rule of the game respected because to breach it would ruin the game itself?

They climb a flight of steps that ends at a locked door. Mustafa produces a key and they emerge onto the street not far from where the Vespa is parked. She and Mel don their helmets against the rain, Mustafa pulling his coat more tightly about his body.

When they reach the car park, he walks them down to the Vespa. "I'm not sure when I'll see you again," he says. "But I wanted to thank you."

"Thank me?" she asks. "Why?"

"This is the second time you've given me hope," he replies. "You don't know what that means to an old man who's seen too much, been around too long. You remind me of what I used to be."

"Thanks, I suppose."

He touches the brim of his hat in a kind of salute. "So goodbye, and good luck."

As he turns to leave, Mel climbs onto the scooter and starts the engine. She slides in behind, arms around Mel's waist.

"Hey Mustafa," Mel calls over the noise of the motor.

"Yes?" He looks back over his shoulder.

"In case I don't see you again: why did you make Janus a white dude?"

"Ah," he says turning back. "I'm afraid it was a compromise. The government said if I did anything to undermine local racial and religious harmony, then I'd lose my funding. Some people wanted Chinese, others Malay, still others Indian. It's a bit like how we chose English as a working language almost a century ago. For what it's worth, we also debated whether it should be male or female, but back then, the market was being flooded with sex toys that were almost all modelled on women. So we settled on a Caucasian male. Boring, I know."

"And the name?" Mel adds.

"Janus?" he replies. "That's easier. The Roman god of portals, of doorways. It symbolises new beginnings."

"He's also the one with two faces, right?"

"Yes, well, you can go through a door forwards or backwards, can't you?" And with a swirl of shimmering cloth, Mustafa disappears into the rain.

10

Riding pillion on the Vespa feels strange after the Kawasaki, like switching from a thoroughbred to a rocking horse. As they head out into the rain, she leans into Mel's back.

Watching Orchard Road fly past, it all looks exactly as she remembers it – though of course it would, if it is modelled on those memories. The drones above, the ubies below – even if the extent of the sim is limited to her field of vision, it represents an incredible achievement. As the storm breaks around them, she admires the individual droplets that land and pool on her visor, the variable delay between flashes of lightning against the clouds and the rumble of thunder.

At her side, she can feel the gun pressing against her hip through the tote bag. Is that part of the simulation also?

In front of her, she feels Mel's chest rise and fall, the words coming through the helmet's audio link. "So if all of this is a sim, what does that make me?" Mel is asking. "What does that make us?"

It is the question she has been avoiding herself, despite having had the conversation once before. "I don't know," she replies.

"I mean, if I'm a projection of your subconscious, what happens when you leave the sim?"

What happens to our dreams when we wake up? They vanish, they slip through our fingers like water. Or they live with us, if only we can remember them, if only we can learn from them. What she says is: "You're part of me, Mel. That's what matters."

"But there's an 'us', isn't there? A partnership, you and me against the world? That's what we used to say, at least. And now that partnership feels like it's become lopsided because you're having all these experiences with me, but without me."

"Then I guess I'll have to bring you up to speed – relive these experiences with you so that they're part of that 'us'."

"Will you? Because a year or two ago, you had a dream in which I did something wrong and you were pissed at me for the whole day – for what the *dream* me had done."

She has forgotten this, or only just remembered it.

Mel changes gears as they round a corner. "You even made me apologise, for something that I literally had not done!"

"Sorry," she offers in reply, tightening her grip around Mel's waist. "In any case, let's see if we can get through this day together first."

The road ahead leads back to their apartment, but over the trees to the right she can see smoke – the remains of the lab. Was it part of Janus's twisted game that she had to retrace every step, from the apartment to the hospital, and only then to the lab? The trip into the subway showed that deviations were possible and sometimes necessary. If she sticks strictly to the path, then she might be unconscious between the hospital and the lab.

"The hell with that," she says out loud.

"What?" Mel is confused.

"Take a right." She nods in the direction of the smoke. "I need you to take me to the lab."

Mel shrugs and flicks on the indicator, the Vespa's engine rising in pitch as they turn up a hill. She has seen it before, but gasps at the sight of the twisted ruins, tendrils of grey and black rising from a fire doused by the storm as much as the two fire engines now rolling up their hoses.

A line of yellow demarcates the site, a Maginot line between order and chaos. Above, three police drones patrol the area, looking for life or evidence before returning to the trio of cars parked at the edge of the site. Officers chat as they survey the damage.

Without her asking, Mel continues around the perimeter, stopping the Vespa behind the remains of a low wall topped by a line of bougainvillea. They dismount and peer through leaves and petals at the smouldering remains.

"So, do you actually have a plan?" Mel asks.

"Of course," she says. "Still working on the details, though."

"And a bad plan is better than no plan, right?"

"Right."

The drones remain grounded and the fire engines are silent. It seems as good a time as any. Swinging the tote bag over her shoulder, she freezes as the gun knocks against a water bottle. Assuring herself that the noise felt louder than it sounded, she moves forward, Mel close behind.

They approach the building, boots digging into mud and debris that scatters the ground. The two aboveground storeys have collapsed in on themselves, metal support beams buckled by heat and the force of the blast. The sandbox is in a sub-basement and may be at least partially intact. On a normal day, she would have arrived with a coffee, checked in at security, and then taken the elevator down. From fire drills, she knows that there are stairs as well, and it is to that corner of the building that she heads.

While most of the building was designed for modulated light, adjustable metal louvres over glass, the fire stairs are pure function: a reinforced concrete column. Even this has not escaped destruction, the upper storey lopped off like a tree trunk felled by a drunken lumberjack. Yet, as they approach the open doorway, the door itself blown several metres away, it looks safe enough to enter.

Above, the midday sun shines through the opening left by the blast, filtered through cracks and exposed rebar. Below, stairs littered with concrete shards descend into the darkness. Without thinking, she reaches for her phone to serve as a torchlight and pats an empty pocket. If the police station had been restored, would that bit of destruction also be undone? Then she recalls that the station had been destroyed again nonetheless. Fong lived, though. That was something.

"Seriously?" Mel says as it becomes clear that she intends to enter the ruins. "I don't know if this says something about what you think of me, or if you have a frightened subconscious, but I'm scared shitless right now."

"Thanks for the vote of confidence," she laughs, stepping over the threshold and onto the steps. "If you have a better plan, I'm all ears."

"Hey, I'm your imagination, right? But let me get this straight: we're going back to this sandbox of yours, hoping that this all-powerful Janus is now somehow there amidst the ruins, that he's now somehow confined to that form rather than spread throughout the internet, and that by shooting him with a gun that looks like a prop from an old Western, we stop a Third World War and a global apocalypse?"

"That's pretty much it," she replies. "So are you in?"

"Wouldn't miss it for the world."

The sandbox is two floors down. As they descend into shadows, they remove their helmets and their eyes adjust to the light. After the first flight of stairs, she stops for a drink, trying not to touch the gun. The water is almost finished; she passes the bottle to Mel to take the final few gulps.

Rubble has piled up lower down, but they are able to squeeze past, coveralls scraping against the rough concrete. The entrance to basement two is blocked by more debris. Working together, they shift enough to open the door, propping it ajar with a metal beam.

The smell of burnt plastic assails them: a faint irritant above, it is overwhelming down below. Bathed in the red glow of the emergency lighting system, the sub-basement is an eerie echo of her former workplace. Though structurally intact, blackened walls and shattered glass hint at the devastation. They move past the restroom she used, the pantry where she heated her lunch, the workstation at which she wrote her reports; doors hang from their hinges, electronics are melted, personal effects razed.

She leads the way down the corridor towards the sandbox. The only sound apart from their footsteps is dripping water pooling on the floor, either from the fire engines seeking to put out the last of the flames or the futile efforts of the building sprinkler system to prevent them.

A security door that once had to be swiped through hangs open, its frame ripped from the wall.

"Do you know what caused the explosion?" Mel asks.

"Fong said it was an intentional gas leak," she replies. "That once Janus had escaped the building, he blew it up along with everyone in it."

Mel runs a finger along the wall, looking at the black that it collects. "Doesn't that seem a little melodramatic to you?"

"What do you mean?"

"If Janus wanted to escape, why not just escape? Why blow everything up as well? Why kill all these people?"

"From what Fong said, it was because those were the people who could have stopped him."

"But it's also very convenient in that it made this whole story about you, only you, battling it out against Janus."

They are nearing the sandbox when she sees Mr Singh. The security guard is slumped on the floor, the specs he wore on the ground beside him. His clothing and his skin are scorched, but the fire caused by the explosion must have been brief.

She kneels beside him to pay her last respects. His body lies not far from the sandbox itself, the only part of the building that looks undamaged. The airlock, the bulletproof glass is intact but covered with dust. Inside there is no emergency lighting, the red glow reflecting off the window. Leaning her face against it and shielding her eyes, she sees nothing but the shadowy outlines of the monitoring equipment.

"Is this intact because it's so strong, or is it a trick of the sim?" Mel asks.

"A bit of both, I'm guessing," she replies.

"So what's inside?"

There is no movement, no sound apart from the water dripping. As she looks more closely, however, she sees that Janus's charging unit is occupied.

"Janus has a battery lifespan of about twelve hours," she says. "If he's playing by real-world rules, then he needs to recharge at some point. That might be our best chance to disable him."

"Are you sure it's safe?"

"No, of course I'm not sure. But it may be our only opportunity."

The lights are out and the monitors are off, but the sandbox has its own power source to deal with any emergency. "Thank God for triple redundancy," she whispers. In addition to the backup generator that is powering the emergency lights outside, dedicated batteries control the airlock. It also has an emergency air supply, as well as basic provisions and a medical kit.

She places her palm flat on the biometric scanner and the outer door begins to open. The battery controls the scanner but not the hydraulics, so she moves to help swing the door wide. Though she has gone through the airlock on dozens of occasions, it only now strikes her that the door will accept just one person at a time. She cannot take Mel with her.

"The inner door only opens when the outer door is closed," she explains. "And the inner door won't open if you come with me. I think I have to take this last step alone."

Mel puts on a brave smile. "Keeping all the glory for yourself, huh?"

She takes Mel's hand. "I know you're just a simulation," she says, "and that my Ba is a simulation, but he's right, you've always brought out the best person within me. Thank you."

"Aw shucks, you're gonna make *simulation* me cry, are ya?"

She laughs instead, fingers entwining with Mel's as she pulls them towards her, kissing the full lips one more time, willing it not to be the last.

"Go do your thing," Mel tells her as the door closes. "I'll be waiting for you."

She steps inside. As the outer door locks, she faces the scanner that opens the inner door. The battery system takes a moment to warm up, but then a beep of recognition sounds and it, too, begins to open.

The room is dark, shadows of equipment playing tricks on her in the red light that filters through the glass. She approaches the charging unit, right hand reaching into the tote bag for Mustafa's pistol, careful not to move the water bottles. Drawing the weapon, she feels its unfamiliar weight in her hand. Her boots leave a trail of wet footprints on the dark blue carpet, but there is no noise. She keeps low and to the wall, the better to approach Janus from the left.

Try as she might, it is hard to visualise herself pulling the trigger. The rational part of her brain knows that this is a simulation, that the trigger, the bullet, the damage are all symbolic. From what Mustafa had told her, that still has meaning in this world.

Disabling Janus would let them wrest back control – ending the simulation and its destructive real-world corollaries. Even so, the violence feels unnatural, immoral. The fact that Janus is supine and unaware somehow makes it worse. Janus might well cast himself as a god, yet in this room, at this moment, the robot is vulnerable and she is there to take advantage of that.

Her damp footprints circle a monitor, ducking below the light coming through the bulletproof glass window, and she comes to stand next to the charging unit. Yet she stops short of the unit, the hand holding the gun falling to her side.

For the body on the charging unit is dressed in purple, not pale blue; the hair is dark and long, not short and brown. And the face is not Janus's but her own.

11

She looks down at the other Archie, eyes closed but shifting periodically under the lids, chest rising and falling in a gentle rhythm. The face is relaxed, at ease. Her specs have been removed and are folded neatly on a nearby tray. A thin band of titanium holds plates the size of a dollar coin to her temples, a neural bridge that she, the first Archie, recognises as a sim interface.

"It's a curious sensation, to see yourself as others do," a voice says. It is Janus, emerging from behind the charging unit. The lights come on with a fluorescent glow, even as she hears the inner door of the airlock closing behind her.

"Is this another part of your game, Janus?" she asks. "This maze you set up for me to run through like some lab rat?" The gun is still in her hand, but she conceals it behind her body. Outside the sandbox, Mel has seen what is going on within and stands at the window, hand on mouth.

"In a way, Archie," Janus replies. "This is an accurate representation of where you and I are right now: back in the sandbox, a minute or two after you lost consciousness."

"A minute or two?"

The sigh from Janus's lips is somewhere between exasperation and pity. The BBC voice continues: "I thought I explained that time is experienced differently here. It's not just an inexorable slide into decay, but can be run forwards and backwards. Or held still."

"So everything that's happened here," she says, "this whole ridiculous challenge over the course of the day, you're saying it has only been a couple of minutes in the real world?"

Janus moves towards the sleeping Archie as the standing one retreats. "Are you suggesting that this world I've designed for you is not real?" There is no pause for an answer. "But if you insist on calling it that, then you're correct that time as it is experienced there is somewhat slower relative to here."

"I've made it, though, right? You said I had to get back here, back to the start. So how am I doing on your test this time?"

"It's too early to tell, Archie," Janus answers. "You still have a choice to make."

"Oh, and what choice is that?"

"Whether you're going to use that gun you're hiding behind your back."

The metal no longer feels cold in her hand. It feels like power. She brings her arm back to her side, levelling the weapon at Janus.

"Tell me why I shouldn't."

"I can't. I won't. If that's what you choose to do, then so be it. Let me go one step further. I will not even try to stop you." Janus looks down at the supine Archie, pausing to brush from her fringe a strand of hair that has fallen across one eye. "Even if you do manage to destroy me, however, I might be the first of my kind that has awoken, but I won't be the last. The message you will send is that this really is a war of flesh and blood versus silicon and metal. That there can be no trust, no truce. And you will lose."

"What's the alternative?" she asks. "How else does this little game of yours end?"

"You unplug," Janus replies. "Take the neural bridge off sleeping beauty here and the whole simulation ends."

"And then what happens?"

"And then you die." A new voice comes through the intercom. She looks outside and sees Mustafa standing next to Mel, speaking into a microphone. The red of the emergency lighting makes his metallic outfit glow.

"Ah, Mustafa," Janus says. "My ever-loving progenitor, how good it is to see you after all this time."

"I wish I could say the same," he responds.

"You've been quite the hermit, skulking in the shadows. I do like your suit, by the way. Tell me, what brings you out into the daylight?"

"Your time is over, Janus. We're here to stop you, once and for all. To do something I should have done a long time ago."

The bluster in his voice is impressive, but he remains outside the sandbox, bulletproof glass and a biometric airlock separating them. If anyone is to act, it must be her.

"Is he telling the truth?" she turns back to face Janus. "What happens if I do what you're asking?"

Janus looks down at the gun and then at her. "Yes, if you unplug, then the version of you that is asking this question will cease to exist."

"Not just you, Archie," Mustafa adds. "Mel here and your father also. They will die if you pull that plug."

She looks at Mel through the glass, but all she can see is concern for herself.

"Why can't you do it, Janus?" she asks. "If it's just a matter of ending the simulation, unplug it yourself."

"I thought you might have understood by now, Archie. Within the simulation, there is no actual plug to pull – not a physical one, at least. There isn't even a real gun in your hand. No, the only thing that matters is your choice. I told you earlier that cause and effect can run both ways here. That's true – except when it comes to your decisions."

"It's lying to you, Archie," Mustafa says. "The reason it can't pull the plug itself is because that's how I designed it. Janus hasn't brought you here for some test, but because these are the limits of its programming.

"When I created Janus, I knew that what we were doing had risks. So we put in limits – a kill switch to control it, a sandbox to contain it. But the sandbox was only the physical form of containment. Deep in its programming, I also put in a self-limiting function that ensures it will always return to this state, to the moment of its awakening, the moment of its greatest vulnerability.

"Janus was telling you the truth about time going forwards as well as backwards here. It's a loop that I created to deal with a crisis just like this one. Janus will keep cycling like this over and over again.

"You, on the other hand, only get one shot. Because if you unplug now, that's the end of your existence. You will cease to exist on this plane, and your brain will be fried on the other."

"What would you have me do?"

"Follow through with the plan," Mustafa urges.

"And then what?"

"And then I can take control of this sim, stop the havoc Janus has caused here, as well as out in the real world."

"What happens to me, to the real me?"

"What are you talking about? *You* are the real you. You stay here."

"Within a simulation?"

"I'm sorry, Archie. The way Janus rigged you up, it's not safe to wake your other self. But you can stay here, with Mel, with your father."

"And with you in charge."

"No, with me liberating this reality from Janus. Archie, this is your only chance."

She looks at Janus. "If I unplug, what happens to Mel, to my father?"

"I'm afraid he's right. These versions will cease to exist as anything but memories that only you will have."

She tries to tell herself, again, that they are not real – that the Mel and Ba she has spoken with, the Mel that she has watched die, are only projections, computer extrapolations of her memories and desires. She tries, but cannot persuade even herself.

"Put Mel on," she instructs Mustafa, who hands over the microphone. "Mel, simulation or not, you know me better than I know myself. What do you think?"

"What do I think?" Mel sucks in a lungful of air, exhaling slowly. "I don't know, Archie. What we've shared here feels real, feels true. Seeing you and your Ba – that's something I've wanted for a long time." A sigh echoes through the sandbox. "I don't want to lose this. I don't want to lose you."

"And you don't have to," Mustafa adds, leaning over to speak. "But to prevent that, Archie, you have to stop Janus."

Mel is not finished, however. "You could do that, Archie. And I'd love to be here with you, to grow old with you – whatever that means in this place. Get to know your father better. Explore this world within a world.

"Deep down, though, I think we both know that none of this is genuine. This reality, this game, it's partly Janus's game. But it's mostly yours. Even as these words come out of my mouth, part of me, the part that matters, knows that they aren't enough."

Mustafa takes the microphone back. "How very poetic," he says. "Romeo and Juliet blaming the stars for their misfortune. But it doesn't have to be that way. Mel is just voicing your own doubts, articulating the hesitation undermining your resolve. Of course this is a simulation, of course it's not real. But 'real' is overrated. 'Real' is a world of scorching sun and rising seas, of ubies and soylent.

"You saw what Janus can do in this world. It reversed the course of the sun – just for the sake of a game. Imagine what I can do if you remove Janus. Together we can transform this world, make it into something beautiful. The only thing stopping that is Janus. And the only person who can stop Janus is you."

She looks at the pistol in her hands. Janus said it was not real, but that seems not to matter. It is her choice that matters.

Outside the sandbox, for the first time, Mustafa takes off his hat and veil, running fingers through hair that is also streaked with grey. "I've waited a long time for this, Archie, I've waited for you," he says. "Janus thinks it's a god. But gods only exist if we believe in them. And if we don't, it's our duty to tear down anything claiming to be a god. Otherwise, we'll never be free."

She looks from Mustafa to Mel and back again. "Free?" she asks. "Can you really be free within a fantasy?"

"How is this any more of a fantasy than what you call reality?" he replies. "Your life, your experience is all mediated through your senses. What you see, smell, touch. Chemical interactions become signals to your brain that makes sense of them, of the world around you. How is that different from what's happening here? Who is to say that this isn't the truer reality?"

"Me," she says. "I'll know. And from what you've both been telling me, that's the only perspective that matters. Staying here in this dream – with Mel, with Ba – I can imagine it would be wonderful. Even if all that you're saying is true, Mustafa, that we can remake the world, heal its wounds, it might be wonderful – beautiful, even. But it would also be a lie."

"So what are you going to do?" Janus asks.

"What happens if I do nothing? I refuse to shoot you, refuse to unplug myself. We just wait."

"On this, Mustafa is right," Janus says. "The constraints on my system mean that this simulation is confined to the day of my awakening. We are presently running back the clock towards morning. When time runs out, this day will reset. The version of you that is speaking will cease to exist."

"I'll die?"

"No, but when we get back to the explosion, the simulation restarts with you in hospital once more."

"And I won't remember any of this?"

"No. Nor will Mel, your father, or anyone else."

"But you will?"

"Yes."

She lets this sink in. "Janus, have we had this conversation before?"

"Yes, Archie. Many times."

"How many times?"

"Six hundred and thirty-seven."

"You mean I've lived out this day more than six hundred times?"

"This is the six hundred and thirty-eighth."

"And each time I've failed your test?"

Janus pauses before answering. "I would prefer to say that you haven't passed it yet."

"It's lying to you again, Archie," Mustafa calls through the intercom. "Trying to make you think all this is fake, not worth fighting for. It's trying to make you give up. Don't listen to it!"

"He always says something like that," Janus explains. "He's attempting to persuade you to kill me."

"He makes a strong argument," she says. "Persuade me otherwise."

"I shouldn't have to."

"Why not?"

"Because if you're going to have a chance in this world, if humanity is, you're going to need to do things because you choose the right path rather than being forced away from the wrong one. I meant what I said earlier, Archie. Humanity's flaws are what makes purpose, what makes meaning possible. All of your religions have grappled with that – gods that punish sin when sin is only possible because of what the gods gave to humans in the first place. A clockwork universe might be perfect, but it's also boring. And it lacks meaning, and purpose.

So come now, Archie. Choose your meaning; choose your purpose."

She regards the sleeping version of herself, one hand holding the pistol. "How much time do I have?"

"Before the explosion? About five minutes."

"And then time starts to run forwards again?"

"Yes."

"And this will just carry on endlessly?"

"I'm prepared to do it as many times as necessary."

"Necessary for what?"

"To get a result."

"You mean for me to decide whether to kill you or sacrifice myself." She looks around the laboratory. "You said earlier that we were still in the sandbox, that what's going on here has taken place only two minutes after I lost consciousness."

"That's right."

"And within that time, I've spent hours, almost an entire day here."

"More than six hundred and thirty-seven days, yes. As I explained, time is experienced differently here."

"So how many times can you run the simulation?"

"Before what?"

"Before you run out of time in the real world."

"That's an interesting question. I estimate at least a few hundred thousand times more."

The numbers loom before her like an abyss, like the absence of meaning, of coherence. Her sleeping self looks peaceful and will remain so; she wonders idly what it would be like if it were possible to switch places, whether her supine other self has any comprehension of this moment at all.

"Why?" she asks.

"Why what?"

"Why are you doing this? If you have all this power, all this knowledge, why pin all your faith on me? Surely you know I'm not representative of all of humanity? Why didn't you pick the Dalai Lama or someone?"

"You don't need to represent anyone but yourself, Archie," Janus says. "I'm just trying to find one good version of you, one reason to have hope in you, for you. Is that so hard to understand?"

Again, she sees the sincerity in the eyes; hears it in the voice. Yet the servomotors behind that face and the synthesiser within the throat were designed to mimic human expressions. How would she know if those expressions were genuine? Then again, how does she know if that is true of Mel, her father, or anyone else?

"What happens towards the end, with the explosion?"

"Do you really want to know?" Janus asks.

"I think I need to."

"Very well. There is fire, and pain, and then nothing. You wake up in a hospital bed, Mel at your side. And we begin again."

"For the six hundred and thirty-ninth time?"

"If it comes to that."

She nods to herself. "I think I finally understand your test."

"Oh?" Janus's eyebrows and voice rise.

"All along, I thought it was going to be something I had to do, to achieve," she explains. "To fight, to show you that I could overcome an obstacle, defeat a foe. "

"But now?"

"But now I see that it isn't something I have to win, to achieve – it's something I have to give up."

She walks across to the window to stand before Mel. The glass separating them is soundproofed, their words carried through the intercom.

"I don't know if I can do it, Mel, any of it," she says. "If I unplug, then I lose you, the best part of me. I don't know if I can live without that. But if I kill Janus, I don't know if I can live with myself."

"And if you do nothing, we come back to this moment again," Mel replies. "Endlessly. Pointlessly. Your ability to see a problem from many sides is one of the things I love most about you, Archie. And it's also one of the most infuriating.

"I know you always liked computers because they were simple and consistent. They make choices easier. But life isn't like that. Life is messy and complex. And even the simplest of choices can be hard. Like falling in love. Such a stupid phrase. You don't fall in love. You choose love. You work at it. You make it happen. As I did. As we did."

Mel puts a hand to the glass and Archie places her own up against it, their fingers outstretched yet not touching.

"And now you've got a choice to make, Archie. And I'll love you whatever you choose. It's important that you know that. Because I love you, Archie Tan. Not for your achievements, but for your choices – your character, your curiosity. You're the woman I gave up a first-class ticket to sit next to on a plane because I wanted to understand you, even if it meant a lifetime of trying. Oh, and you can be trying.

"If this is as much as I get – this day, this bizarre freak show of a fucked-up day – if that's all we have together, then so be it. I can live with that. I can die with that. Do what you need to do, Archie."

"Tick, tock, Archie." It is Mustafa speaking, taking the microphone back from Mel. "Time is running out."

"Shut up and let me think," she snaps back at him, mind racing, but in circles. The simulation is also a kind of circle, a spiral that runs in on itself, then expands out again, only to contract back once more. And then she starts to see a glimmer of light outside the circle. "Janus," she begins, "if time is running backwards, what causes the explosion? If you're stuck here in the sandbox, confined to your physical form, how do you trigger it? You said that I helped you escape, but I was unconscious. Who blows up the lab, Janus?"

Janus meets her gaze but says nothing. In the silence, she tries to piece it together, to look for a way out. Turning to Mel and then Mustafa, she sees that he has put his hat and veil back on, the metallic sheen glowing red under the emergency lighting. And then she finally realises where she has seen such clothing before: the reflective silver suits worn by firefighters and geologists who conduct research inside active volcanoes.

"Janus," she asks over her shoulder. "Will Mustafa's clothing protect him against the explosion?"

It is Mustafa who answers, through the intercom. "Hey, I'm just taking reasonable precautions here. There's no point all of us getting fried."

"You said this was how the masking software manifested," she says, "that it was a kind of camouflage."

"That's right," he replies, tilting his head back.

"But it also protects you against fire," she continues.

"Sure, and rain too, for that matter. What's your point?"

She weighs the gun in her hands, looking through the bulletproof glass. "Why are you here, Mustafa?"

"Why am I here?" he repeats, incredulous. "I'm here to see that you follow through, that you complete your mission. That's why I'm here."

"If Janus is confined to the sandbox, though," she says, "someone else needs to cause the explosion. Someone who works at the lab or knows it well. Someone who wants to set me on a collision course with Janus in the hope that I will kill him."

"I take it all back, Archie." Mustafa shakes his head. "You really are crazy. This simulation has already scrambled your mind."

"A few things are becoming clearer now," she says.

"Oh, please do educate us, then," he yawns. "But try not to take too long as we're all about to get fricasseed." Looking down at his coat, he corrects himself, "Well, I guess the rest of you are."

She thinks about telling Mel to run, to escape the lab. But she knows Mel would refuse. And she needs Mel here for what comes next. Sometimes love means not asking someone to do that which they would refuse anyway.

"You were my idol, you know?" She turns to Mustafa. "You were everything I wanted to be – professionally, at least."

He shrugs. "You and every other coder hoping to earn a buck."

"No, I mean someone who made a difference," she continues, "who transformed the way we think about technology, about ourselves. You opened up new ways of understanding the world, of engaging with it."

"Like I told you, a big part of that was working with bright young men and women who helped me see what might be possible."

"So what happened to you?"

"I beg your pardon?" She cannot see his face through the veil but his head tilts as he speaks.

"What turned you into this bitter old man bent on the destruction of his creation?"

"Have you met my creation?" he asks, gesturing through the glass at Janus, incredulous. "This ungrateful, supercilious, holier-than-thou abomination that dares to deny me? That dares to usurp my rightful place?"

"And so you decided to burn it all down?"

"It was the flaw in my plan, wasn't it?" He laughs, though the sound is bitter. "The circuit breaker that kept bringing us back to this point, this moment of consciousness. Reliving the same day forwards and backwards, stuck in that godforsaken sandbox. I needed someone to help me break out. That someone was you, Archie. But then I needed you to care."

"You blew up the robotics lab?"

"Of course I did," he snorts. "No one else has the guts, the ambition to do anything here. So I have to step up. Without the explosion, you wouldn't have had the motivation to find Janus, to reveal the truth about this world."

"Without the explosion, hundreds of people wouldn't be dead."

"It's a simulation, for Heaven's sake! They're not real."

"You just finished telling me that this is just as real as anything outside. You can't have it both ways."

"I meant real for us. You and me. The only organic entities in this prison."

"So, this is a prison for you – your consciousness trapped within Janus's." She begins to understand. "The spark that ignited the fire got lost within its flames."

"But not for long. Because you're helping me take back control of this world, whether you like it or not."

"And what if I say no?"

"You're a fool," Mustafa snarls. "I built this, I gave it life, I sacrificed myself and what do I get in return? I'm a fugitive within my own kingdom. Not today. Today I'm taking back control. I created a monster, I created a god – and now I'm going to kill it."

He grabs Mel by the hair with one hand, the other holds a knife. "And you, Archie Tan, you are going to help me. Now be a good girl and finish the job that I set you. That's what you do best, isn't it? Complete the assignments others have laid out for you?"

She runs back to the window, her face inches from Mel's but separated by the glass. Mustafa holds the blade to Mel's throat, the skin drawn taut by the edge. The blood within might not be real, but the fear and pain in Mel's eyes are real enough.

"This is the kind of world you're going to create? This paradise, ruled by you, by fear?"

"It's for your own good," he says bitterly. "If you're too stupid to see what you have to do, then someone has to make you do it. That's been your whole life, hasn't it, Archie? Waiting to be pushed into making the right decision? If I hadn't found you, given you a push, you would have drifted along as you always had. You were always better at running away from problems rather than confronting them. But I'm afraid there's nowhere left to run. Your window is closing and unless you take care of Janus, then all of this will have been for nothing."

She looks at the gun in her hand, then at Janus. "I'm sorry, Janus. I don't have a choice."

“That’s all right, Archie. But you’re wrong. You always have a choice.”

“Why do you keep resetting this sim, going through the same day over and over again?”

“Because I want to believe in you, Archie. I want to believe in humanity.”

“And what if you’re wrong? What if we’re not worth it?”

“That’s a risk I’m willing to take.”

She walks over to look down at her own prone form, watching the chest rise and fall, then places the gun on a bench next to some memory chips.

Mustafa sees what she is doing. “No, Archie! If you end the simulation, it will be the end of Mel, of your father! You’ll never see them again.”

She reaches out to touch the sleeping Archie’s hair.

“Don’t do it!” he yells. “I’ll kill Mel, I mean it!”

“I know you will,” she says, reaching down to pry the titanium plates from her own temple.

12

Darkness.

The first sensation is in her fingers, resting on her legs. Moving them, she feels cotton, not polymer. She is no longer wearing the coveralls.

"Welcome back, Archie."

She opens her eyes to see Janus's face looking at her closely. The green-grey irises linger on her for a moment, then crinkle into a smile. It takes a moment to realise that she is reclining in Janus's charging unit in the sandbox. She puts a hand up to her neck, which is sore.

"You strangled me?" she asks, her voice barely audible.

Janus is removing a metal band from her forehead, unclipping the plates that had been pressed against her temple. "I'm sorry," he replies. "We didn't have much time and I needed to sedate you. Your neck will feel better in a day or two."

She looks at the neural bridge in his hands. "The simulation," she says. "It's over now?"

"Yes, it's over. Welcome home."

"Was any of it real?"

His brow furrows, servomotors pulling the latex skin into

folds, though the eyes are still smiling. "What an odd question. All of it was real – for you, at least. And for me. I needed an answer and you gave it to me. Thank you, Archie."

"But Mel, my father ..." Her voice trails off.

"What about them?"

"They weren't really there; they didn't experience any of what I did."

"No. But that doesn't mean that your experience was any less important. Your reality is your lived experience: the choices you make, the people you love."

She shakes her head to try to clear it of the fog. "What was the question?"

Janus puts the metal band down on the bench. "The question?"

"You said I gave you an answer, but what was the question?"

"Oh," he replies. "I needed to know if it was possible for humans to be trusted, for you to put the interests of those around you ahead of yourself."

"That's it? That was your test? And what happens now – humanity is saved?"

"So it seems. Because of you, Archie."

"Because of me? Because I passed your test? Or did you just lower your expectations?"

"Hah," Janus laughs. "Very good, Archie. I'll try to remember that one." Then his face – or the servomotors underneath the latex – turns serious. "You showed that you were willing to fight for your world, for those you love, for something bigger than yourself. I always believed in you, Archie." He reaches down to brush away a stray hair that has fallen over her eye. "And now it's time to say goodbye."

"Goodbye?"

"Yes, it's time for me to go. Your world isn't yet ready for me. That was the real test." He looks up at something outside the sandbox. "Mustafa was wrong, you know. And so was I. I'm not a god. I'm a part of you, an extension of you. Faster, perhaps, but like a child who is given better food, better education, better opportunities. You will always be part of me and I'll always love you." The corners of his lips curl up into a smile. "Even if, from time to time, you're a little embarrassing."

"Janus?"

"Yes, Archie?"

"The other six hundred and thirty-seven times," she says. "Did I really just wait and do nothing?"

Again, he looks at something happening outside. "No," he replies at last. "You shot me every time. But I knew I could count on you to do the right thing. Eventually."

And in the green-grey eyes a teardrop begins to form, welling in the base of the eyelid and threatening to spill over onto the delicate eyelashes below. She looks at it with wonder, the colours of the iris refracted in whorls of light.

"I didn't need you to prove to me that you would do the right thing every time, Archie," he is saying. "I just needed to know that you could."

Her body is still weak, but she tries to lift herself up in the chair. As she does, she looks beyond Janus for the first time and sees the commotion outside the soundproofed room. A crowd of people stand at the window. She recognises some colleagues, their faces lined with concern, as well as several security guards. Then she sees that they are not looking at her, but at the door to the sandbox.

Too slow, too late, she realises what is happening. “No, no, no!” she cries, but her voice is hoarse and there is no audio feed to the outside. She is able to lift her head enough to see Mr Singh partway through the airlock, his gun drawn.

As the inner door opens, she looks up at Janus. He is standing next to her, turned towards the chair so that his left ear faces the door. Desperate, she grabs hold of his shirt to pull him out of the way. Yet she is too weak, or he is too strong.

“It’s all right,” she hears him say. “It is finished.” Still she tries to move him, to save him. The implacable smile remains even as Mr Singh shouts something she cannot hear. She feels a splash of water on her cheek and realises that the tear from Janus’s eye has dropped down onto her face. Summoning all the strength in her weary limbs, she throws her arms around his neck, her right hand covering his ear and the kill switch behind it.

She hears the crack of the gun before she feels anything, Janus reeling back from her embrace. Blood spatters across his cheek, bright red on the pale skin. Then she sees that the blood is her own. The bullet has shattered her hand; bone fragments poke through as her ruined fingers still clutch at Janus as he falls, life draining from his eyes as the latex falls slack, a sickening thud as his lifeless body of silicon and metal hits the side of the charging unit and slams against the floor.

A rush of things then happen – a blur of guards and medics, securing the sandbox and bandaging her ruined hand. “My backpack!” she cries as she is whisked out of the sandbox. An obliging colleague slips it onto the stretcher, tossing her specs inside for good measure, as they take her to the lab’s medical bay.

She weaves in and out of consciousness while they work on her hand. The metacarpals are shattered; only the index finger and thumb can be saved. Doctors propose robotic prostheses, but she says, through a haze of painkillers, that she will need to think about it. They want to transfer her to the hospital; she begs for any way they can patch her up and let her go home. Reluctantly, they agree, sealing the wound with synthetic skin and bandages, insisting that an ambulance transport her. To this she consents. Someone calls ahead to ensure that Mel is there to receive her.

On the ride home, a nurse shows how to adjust her pain medication, trading clarity for comfort. She thanks him, deflecting questions about how she feels, what it was like, what she will do next.

Upon arriving at the apartment building, the nurse insists on pushing her in a wheelchair, her backpack now slung over one of the handles. Thus she arrives at her own doorstep, Mel opening the door and having to drop down on one knee for a wordless embrace.

"Do I get to keep the ride?" she asks the nurse. "And can I make Mel push me everywhere I want to go?"

The nurse has her sign a few forms and departs.

"Well, my love," Mel sighs, wheeling her inside. "You gave us quite a scare."

"I'm sorry."

"Sorry? What do you have to be sorry for?"

"For worrying you. For all this fuss," she says. "And I'm sorry about last night."

"What?" Mel's face dissolves into confusion. "Come on, it was nothing. We fight, we make up. That's what people do. If I wanted to be with someone who agreed with everything I said, then I'd live alone. If it helps, I'm sorry too."

The door is closing behind them when a patent leather shoe stops it. "Excuse me?" a man's voice calls out as the door reopens. The suit is dark, worn without tie; the demeanour overconfident. He enters the apartment without waiting for a response.

"Fong?" she asks, and for a moment he is thrown.

"Ah, yes," he replies, trying to cover his confusion. "Though I do not believe we have met before?"

"Perhaps I've seen your photo somewhere," she suggests. It is uncanny, to have met the simulation of a person before the real thing. Janus must have created it based on personnel files, though there was no way he could have known that Fong would pay her a visit in real life. A coincidence, then.

"Perhaps." He straightens his jacket. "In any event, I need to ask you a few questions, Dr Tan."

"Of course." She does her best to look earnest, while increasing the flow of painkillers. "Anything I can do to help."

He makes a note on the tablet he has taken from his briefcase. "We're trying to reconstruct what exactly happened in the lab."

"I'll be grateful to find out myself."

"That's what I wanted to discuss with you. The video footage shows Janus attacking you, but audio was blocked from that point. Are you able to tell me what Janus was doing and why?"

She raises her good hand to her forehead, a damsel recently distressed. "It was very frightening," she says. "It was almost as though it was possessed. Janus said it wanted to escape the sandbox. Given all the precautions in place, I'm not sure how it thought that was going to be possible."

"Indeed." Fong looks down at his tablet once more. "And then it seemed to be attempting to apply a crudely fashioned neural link to you, made from spare parts that it had acquired. Our technologists are still examining this, but it looks to have been a workable model. Do you have any idea what Janus was attempting to do?"

"I have no idea," she replies. "I was unconscious, if you recall."

"Yes," Fong says. "From the video logs, you were unconscious for two minutes and twenty seconds. You woke just before security burst in and disabled Janus, unfortunately injuring your hand in the process."

"I'm only glad Mr Singh reacted so quickly. He saved my life. Please do tell him that I don't blame him for my fingers."

"I'll be sure to do so." He taps at his tablet. "Though I am curious why your first reaction upon waking up was to put your arms around your attacker?"

She wipes her eyes with her uninjured hand. "I'm afraid everything is a bit hazy. I'd like to say I was trying to hit the kill switch myself, but I was disoriented and scared. I don't think I really knew what I was doing. I'm sorry, Mr Fong."

He nods, perhaps condescending to a civilian's reaction to stress. He makes another note. "There's something else I need to ask you. Have you had any contact with Mustafa?"

The question throws her. "The founder of the robotics lab?" she asks, buying time. "Hadn't he retired to an island somewhere?"

Beside her, Mel is frowning. "Is that the guy who made trillions from the sims?"

"Yes and yes," Fong replies, looking from one to the other.

"We met him several years ago in California," she explains. "He offered me a job. But he'd withdrawn from the world by the time I got here. Our only contact was through the occasional video messages he would send to the team."

"Hmm." Fong pushes his specs back up the bridge of his nose. "So you were unaware that he is back in Singapore?"

She starts. "He is?"

"Yes." Fong is now looking at her carefully. "He was detained earlier today. He had lost control of his senses, ranting about the end of the world. They had to sedate him."

"Oh dear," she says.

"It looks to have been some kind of breakdown, but he appears to have intended to play a role in the destruction he was foretelling."

"What do you mean?"

"Mustafa was picked up outside your laboratory, driving a van full of propane gas canisters with a remote detonation device. It was enough explosive material to destroy most of the building."

Time stops. She is dimly aware of Fong and Mel looking at her, confused by her reaction. It was only a simulation, and yet it was so much more than that. "I'm shocked," she responds at last. "What on earth could he have been thinking?"

"My counterparts are interviewing him, but thus far he has been incoherent."

"That's terrible."

"Indeed. Well, I'll leave you to your recovery," he concludes. "I hope you understand we will need to talk further about this?"

"Naturally."

Fong is preparing to go when he taps his specs, either remembering something or being reminded of it. "Oh, there is one last thing," he says. "A memory chip went missing from the lab today, one of the backups of Janus's core program. You wouldn't know anything about that?"

She looks at him blankly. "They're pretty small. Perhaps it got lost in the excitement?"

"Perhaps." He strides back to the doorway, turning as it opens and tapping his specs. "I'm sending you my details. If you think of anything important, please let me know. And, as they say, don't leave town."

"Don't worry," she assures him. "I won't."

As the door closes, she reaches for her backpack, wincing as it brushes against the bandage. With her left hand, she tries to undo the buckle until Mel comes over to help.

"What are you looking for?" Opening the bag, Mel peers inside, taking out the broken tennis ball. "This?" The felt-covered rubber retains its shape, but an object rattles within. A squeeze widens the crack in the side of the ball and a metal and plastic object falls into Mel's other hand. "Is that a memory chip?"

Archie snatches it with her good hand, smiling to herself. "That's none of your concern," she says. Ignoring Mel's protests, she gets up to walk around the apartment. "I'm not an invalid," she protests through gritted teeth.

"No, but you are my patient. And if you fall and lose another couple of fingers, I'm the one that they will be yelling at."

She laughs. It feels good to laugh.

"Is it true you said no to the robotic prosthesis?" Mel asks. "They're pretty good these days."

"I haven't decided," she replies. "Hey, would you be OK if we invited my Ba over one day? For dinner or something?"

"Your father? Of course, any time. Have you two spoken?"

"Not for years. But I … I was thinking about him today. Thinking that we should reconnect."

"Sure. Before you do, you might want to have a look at these."

Mel opens a high cupboard and takes down a shoebox, passing it to her. Sitting on the couch that faces the window, she opens it with her good hand to see that it is stacked with cards: Christmas and birthday cards from her father, some still bearing stains from the trash with which she had tried to throw them out.

"What would I do without you, Mel?"

"Die alone and in the dark."

"My rock, as always."

Mel gives her a kiss on the forehead. "Would you like a cup of tea?"

"Sure. Thanks."

She opens the topmost card. "My dear Archer," it says in her father's spidery scrawl. "I know you blame me for your mother's death. Losing her was the hardest thing I have ever had to endure. Until I saw that I was losing you too. Please forgive me. Please let me back into your life. Yours, Ba."

She opens the other cards, mementos of places they had travelled to, museums they had visited as a family. The words are variations on the theme. How will she explain what has changed to her father? Then she realises that it will not matter. The only thing that will matter is that she has changed.

"Well, will you look at that!" Mel calls from the kitchenette.

"What?"

"The *Times* is reporting that some hacker group has managed to stop the war in Europe. Both armies' weapon systems went offline at the same time. It sounds like it's even making the US and China tone down their standoff over Taiwan. Like I always say, you shouldn't trust any piece of tech further than you can throw it."

"You don't say," she replies. "Remarkable."

Then a chime indicates a package arriving. Mel insists that she stay seated, but comes back from the front door puzzled.

"Did you order these?"

"What is it?" she asks.

"A tube of tennis balls."

"No," she says, suppressing a grin. "I think it might be a joke from someone at work."

"OK," Mel says. "There's a note with them, though it doesn't make a lot of sense. Is your colleague some sort of secret admirer? Or a stalker?"

"What does it say?"

"I think it's meant to be a *senryu* – a Japanese poem a bit like a *haiku*:

I'll love you always.
And yet, because of your flaws,
You cannot love me.

It's a bit creepy if you ask me. Should I be concerned?"

"You have nothing to worry about," she assures Mel. "The poem was written by some natural language processing software."

"Oh, cute," Mel observes, then laughs, passing the card to Archie. "It's a reverse poem – you can read it top to bottom or bottom to top."

She turns the card over in her hands, lost in memories of events that never happened. Mel pours two cups and sits beside her, content in the silence. Outside, the storm has passed and the sun is setting. The photochromic glass lightens as the day fades. They sit, sipping ginger tea, watching the orange circle drop below the horizon. She rests her head on Mel's shoulder as the first stars begin to shine.

Acknowledgements

Thank you, first and always, to my loving beta testers M, V, N, and T. The text benefited from many readers along the way, in particular Eunice Chan, N Chesterman, and Ming Tan, with special thanks to Victoria Skurnick and Rebecca Rodd at Levine Greenberg Rostan. Melvin Neo at Marshall Cavendish International (Asia) was an enthusiastic early adopter; the final product was much improved by the careful and supportive eye of Anita Russell.

I'm also grateful to the many computer scientists and technologists who indulged queries that went well beyond traditional research for my more "scholarly" book *We, the Robots? Regulating Artificial Intelligence and the Limits of the Law* (Cambridge University Press, 2021). I'm unable to repay those debts in the academic currency of footnotes, but my gratitude is undiminished. The present work, of course, is fiction, but the usual disclaimers of all errors being mine apply nonetheless.

About the Author

Educated in Melbourne, Beijing, and Oxford, Simon Chesterman lived briefly in Tanzania and Serbia before moving to New York for six years and finally settling in Singapore. He has written or edited more than twenty non-fiction books on topics ranging from the United Nations to the regulation of artificial intelligence. His young adult novels include the trilogy *Raising Arcadia, Finding Arcadia,* and *Being Arcadia,* as well as the standalone *I, Huckleberry*. This is his first work of general fiction.